LIGHT & SHADE

MOSH SERIES BOOK 4

SUSANNA ROGERS

Bucher & Reid

Bucher & Reid

Cover by Amygdala Book Design
978-0-6484920-4-7

ALSO BY SUSANNA ROGERS

MOSH SERIES
Holler & Howl
Down & Dirty
Slash & Burn
Light & Shade
Ride & Crash
Ground & Pound

YOUNG ADULT
Infiltration (Book 1)
Regeneration (Book 2)
Validation (Book 3)

Parallax Error

4

CHAPTER ONE

Joel

Desperation wasn't a good look, not when you wanted something and certainly not when you were dealing with guys who were so damn successful. People could smell it, often from a distance, and it wasn't an attractive aroma.

Act cool, Joel. Yeah, right, like that was going to happen.

It'd been over a month since word had got out that The Merchants' bass player was leaving, a month of putting my feelers out and talking to anyone who even vaguely knew the guys. And waiting. A hell of a lot of waiting.

So when I found out about tonight, I'd jumped at the chance, made sure I got on the invitation list. I'd been playing in bands for ten years, ever since I was seventeen, playing my guts out, shitty gigs and good gigs, always hoping to make it in the music industry even though I had a 'real' job.

This could be my big chance. Maybe my only chance. And I had to make it happen because no one else was going to do it for me.

Lachie Tyler knew how to put on a party, that was for

sure. Once I'd managed to get in. The security guys out front were a bit over the top, but maybe that was what happened when you were famous. Like buying a huge house. It looked like he hadn't gotten around to buying much furniture yet, but the place was so packed with people you could hardly notice.

I'd seen Lachie heading toward the back of the house earlier, so that was where I should go too. Better to do this sooner than later.

I turned. And saw her. Short blond hair, head tilted, and looking right at me. A crimson, off-the-shoulder top showed off pretty shoulders, her arms folded pushing up her boobs, so they might've been staring at me too.

The hair on the back of my neck stood on end. In a good way. The best way possible. All my senses left me, just like that.

"You look like a guy who needs a drink." She swiped a long neck from a passing waiter and shoved it into my hand.

"Thanks."

I drank some beer. Tried to compose myself. Wondered if she'd been watching me. Was it even possible a woman like her could be checking *me* out?

"Nothing tastes as good as free beer." I took another long gulp, embarrassed because that was the best I could come up with, which was weird. Not my normal self at all. Must be nerves. I should speak to Lachie. Soon. Get it over with. Then I'd be back. Oh, yeah, I'd be right back.

She smiled, her warm brown eyes lighting up. "I'm Scarlett."

"Such a pretty name." At least I got one thing right.

A skinny young thing shoved me aside, her arms

outstretched to Scarlett as she dived between us and wrapped her arms around the young woman I'd barely met. Then a guy appeared. Did the same thing.

Scarlett was all smiles, returning their hugs, happy to see them. In fact, she looked like she'd forgotten about me in a few short seconds. Disappointment washed through me.

And brought me to my senses. What was I thinking? This thing with The Merchants could be the chance of a lifetime and I'd gotten so easily distracted. Man, she was one hell of a distraction.

I took a deep breath. I could catch up with her later. In fact, I'd make sure of it. It wasn't every day a woman as stunning as her introduced herself to me. Not every day a woman made me lose my shit either.

No more deliberation. I forced myself to leave, weaving my way through the crowd as I headed toward the back of the house.

Bar staff had set themselves up at the outdoor kitchen. A waiter took my empty beer from me, handed me another one. Like magic. I was going to need it.

Seemed to be more furniture out here than inside the house. A few people had gathered around the outdoor sofas set up to one side of the yard while others were hanging around long tables on the patio. Looked like the perfect place to have a beer with a few friends on a summer's evening like tonight, except in this case there were more than a few friends. The place was filling up.

I liked a party as much as the next guy, but was comfortable on my own too, probably because I'd spent lots of time alone as a kid. Too much. Still, I was better off not living alone and would need to start looking for a new roommate soon.

Deep in conversation with someone, Lachie had his back to me. I swallowed, a fresh wave of anxiety surging through me. I had a lot riding on this.

Should I interrupt? Introduce myself? What if I blew it?

The Merchants of Menace weren't just any band. This was my dream band, what I'd always wanted but had never even dared admit to myself because it seemed too surreal and too far out of my reach.

Now they needed a bass player. This was meant to be. It had to be.

Squealing sounds came from the hot tub at the rear of the yard. "Lachie, Lachie!"

Two naked girls sat up, waving wildly. My eyes nearly popped out of my head. I couldn't believe it. Charlotte Banks. I'd kissed her in the ninth grade, but she hadn't looked like that back then. Talk about way too much information. It felt like my teenage dreams were coming back to haunt me.

Hell, I had to get that image out of my head and do what I'd come out here to do and talk to Lachie Tyler.

He looked away, embarrassed. My big chance. I strode toward him, just a few steps, hard ones to take. Nerves shot through me, my throat suddenly tight.

I shook his hand. "Great party. We've met before."

A blank look on his face. "Have we?"

"Joel Hitchcock." If I'd expected by some miracle he'd remember me, I was wrong. "From Black Paisley." Not even a flicker of recognition from Lachie, so I said, "The band."

Each time I added something, a small piece of my

remaining self-confidence got chipped away. And soon I wouldn't have Black Paisley anymore. One of the guys was leaving, our lead singer was drugged up half the time, and the band was falling apart.

I should've known better. We'd been thrilled Lachie had come along to one of our gigs all those years ago, even if it hadn't been our gig exactly. We'd been the supporting act, and his presence had been a big deal to us. Not to him. And that figured.

Still, I couldn't stop here. I had to at least try, so I told Lachie how I played a bit of guitar and piano and a lot of bass. Shit, I shouldn't have mentioned the other instruments. I should have stuck with the bass because that was the whole point. He was polite though, I had to hand it to him, even told me I was versatile like Nick, their singer.

Despite the compliment, my heart was sinking every step of the way. The look on Lachie's face told me he was going through the motions. Meanwhile the ache inside me deepened, despite the fact I was still hoping for the best, reaching and grasping for this thing I'd never be able to have.

"Lots of guys play bass just so they can get a gig," he said. "Someone told me years ago that if you're a bass player, you'll always get a gig whereas everyone wants to be the guitar player. I reckon that still holds true."

But I played bass because it felt right, because I could write the songs and the bass lines I wanted to play. Because it was me.

I had to give it one last shot. "I, uh, heard you guys might be after a bass player."

Desperation dripped from my voice, so thick even I

could hear it. It pooled inside me too because now I was so close—or so far—it confirmed just how badly I wanted this.

"We might have already found someone," he said.

My stomach plummeted. "Really, who's that?"

"A guy called Domino."

I gritted my teeth. Of all the bass players in the world, of all the musicians in Frankston, they had to choose him.

Lachie raised his eyebrow. "You know him?"

"You could say that."

This was typical. Domino could talk his way into anything. He'd stolen my girlfriend from me, talked his way right into her pants and her heart, and it might've been years ago but I hadn't forgotten. I couldn't.

Anyway, wasn't he in rehab? Or had he just come out? My head spinning, I couldn't even remember.

It took all my strength not to say anything. I'd only make myself look bad. Or worse, I'd end up ranting and that was not a good look. Besides, Lachie didn't know me from a bar of soap and had no reason to believe anything I said, not when he already had a bass player.

I swallowed back the resentment, wondering what the hell to say next.

Scarlett came toward us, gliding through the crowd. She'd stand out anywhere with her pale hair, that bright top, and that attitude. My heart melted at the sight of her. Such magnificent timing.

She greeted Lachie with a kiss on the cheek. A pang of jealousy shot through me. At a kiss on the cheek? Talk about crazy.

"This is some house you've got," she said.

Maybe that was what I should've done too, flattered

Lachie a little, found some common ground. It wouldn't have been hard since I was a huge fan of The Merchants.

Scarlett placed her hands on her hips. "You've got so much house and it's so empty."

Something we agreed on. Then she made a comment about how when all the people were gone she'd bet this place didn't feel like 'him'. Which was what I'd thought earlier too, only she'd put it so much better than I could have.

He grinned, sidled closer to her. "Now how do you know what I feel like?"

Joking, relaxed, teasing. With her, Lachie was all the things he hadn't been with me. I'd done this all wrong and blown it. Maybe I'd been too late anyway.

Scarlett turned and looked at me, probably waiting for an introduction. That was all she did, but it sent my pulse racing.

"Scarlett, this is…" Lachie's voice tapered off.

This is … nobody. This is…

"Joel Hitchcock," I said, my mouth suddenly dry.

"Yes, Joel's a bass player," he added. "With Black Paisley."

What a way to make a lousy impression on a girl. Such a letdown. At least Lachie had remembered the name of the band. It was something.

Scarlett turned to him, asked if he needed an interior architect for his house, didn't push the point.

Then she said, "Nick told me how sick your dad is. I'm sorry to hear it, Lachie."

I'd heard his father had cancer. Maybe I should have mentioned something too but it hadn't seemed right when I barely knew the guy.

She touched Lachie's arm—touched a piece of my heart if I was going to be honest—then apologized for interrupting, as if there'd been anything for her to interrupt. She seemed to know exactly the right thing to say.

"It's okay, really, no problem at all," Lachie said. "But tonight's not for sickness. It's for drinking."

He raised his beer so I clinked my bottle against his and took a sip even though I didn't feel much like drinking anymore.

And I watched Lachie leave, my dreams disappearing with him, dissolving before my eyes. Maybe my vision wasn't as great as Martin Luther King's but I had a dream. Everyone was allowed to dream.

Yep, Lachie had gone, leaving me with a sinking feeling.

And with Scarlett.

CHAPTER TWO

Scarlett

Hell, I really screwed that up, first with Lachie, then with Joel. I couldn't work out what was going on with that guy.

Maybe that was why I'd gone up to him in the first place. Because he was a big question mark. The good looks certainly didn't hurt. Long wavy black hair, dark eyes, exotic features—Indian maybe—and a killer smile even if he wasn't smiling much now. He might have a friendly face but that didn't mean I was going to let him get away with anything.

I held his gaze. "I got you a beer and you abandoned me."

"Abandoned?" He choked on his drink. "Sorry, I didn't think I was deserting you, just leaving you with your friends."

Old school friends who were dying to tell me they'd just got engaged. As much as I was pleased for them, it had been so long since I'd seen them that it was hard to get excited. Also, whether they knew it or not, they'd been interrupting something.

"Yeah, they were a bit OTT," I said.

"Thanks for the beer, though. That was perfect timing."

"Glad to hear it."

I didn't want to think the way to a man's heart was with booze, but it was a start. And maybe I did want to start something with him or at least get to know him a little. Maybe more than a little.

He brought a hand to his ear. "I didn't catch your last name."

"Scarlett Novak."

"Like the actress."

A 1950s movie star, an icy blonde no less, and not at all like me. I hoped he didn't think I was cold or frosty.

"I'm not quite as mysterious and intriguing as her." I held his gaze. "So how do you know Lachie?"

"I don't."

It only made me more curious. Lots of people wanted to party at Lachie Tyler's house, me included, but at least I knew him.

"Then what brings you here?" I asked.

"You really want to know?"

I waited. I really did want to know. Didn't matter that I'd just met him. I wanted to know a lot about Joel Hitchcock.

After a while, he said, "I play bass, and The Merchants need a bass player."

"Ah, so that's it."

A musician, not the answer I wanted to hear. They were way too much hard work. I'd seen what Lily had been through with Nick, the uncertainty, the volatility, and maybe even the ego. Besides, the last thing I needed was to get hurt again after everything I'd been through.

Still, I shouldn't let myself be disappointed when all we were doing was chatting.

I wondered if I should tell Joel my sister was engaged to Nick, their singer. Or wait? I didn't want Joel to suddenly spark up and get excited about talking to me because of who I was related to and how this might help him, not if he wasn't genuinely interested in me. I wasn't the type of gal to take second best, not anymore.

He nodded. "Yep, me and probably about a thousand other people would give their eye teeth to join that band."

"Yeah, I think that's what happens when you're famous. Everyone wants a piece of you."

He smiled. "Do you speak from experience?"

I placed a hand on my chest. "Me? I'm not famous."

"Sure you're not a supermodel in your spare time?"

A come-on line if I'd ever heard one. Still, it made for a little sizzle inside me. Maybe the conversation was heading in the right direction after all.

I shrugged. "You know what it's like. I don't find much time for super-modeling between vacationing in the Bahamas and taking the private jet to dinners with Harry and Meghan at Buckingham Palace."

"Yep, I've got the same problem." He pushed his hair behind his ears so I could better see his face and the dark eyes that sparkled against his coffee-colored skin. "So, I take it you're an interior architect?"

A subject I didn't particularly want to talk about right now, not after my failed efforts to get Lachie on board as a client. When my boss found out about this party, she'd urged me to speak to him about it, since he was rock 'n' roll royalty and one of Frankston's most famous exports. Her words, not mine.

I shouldn't have listened to her, shouldn't have let her push me around, and I should definitely have waited and asked about Lachie's father first. I knew how hard it was to lose your dad. Still, I saw in Lachie's eyes that he'd appreciated my concern even if there was nothing I could do to help.

"Look, my boss insisted I broach the subject with Lachie," I said. "I couldn't get out of it."

"You could've lied." A teasing smile tugged at the corners of Joel's lips. "Gone back to work on Monday morning and pretended you'd asked."

"I'm not a very good liar."

"That's good to know."

"But you don't know that. I could be lying to you right now."

He grinned. "Well, it looks like we were both hoping to get something out of Lachie."

"I guess we were."

"It's a huge bummer." He threw one hand up. "For me anyway. I've played in lots of bands but never one as big as The Merchants. They're really something. I've been doing this so long, and..."

"And?"

He shook his head. "It's such a struggle, something you put your heart and soul into. The highs are high, and the lows are..."

"Low."

"Oh, yeah."

"Black Paisley are popular, though," I said.

"Not quite in the same league." His dark eyes widened. "You've seen us play?"

"A few times."

I'd recognized Joel from the band, of course. Their singer may have been the one who pranced across the stage and put on a show, but that didn't compare with Joel's quiet energy and presence. Yeah, I'd definitely noticed him.

"I think that was why I went up to you earlier," I said. "And handed you a beer. I'd seen you on stage so you seemed kind of familiar even if I didn't know where from at the start."

That killer smile again. Clearly I'd said the right thing.

"Well, that's a definite bonus from playing in a band. I get free beer and I get to meet an attractive woman."

I gave him a sly look. "I bet you meet plenty of those."

He didn't deny it. That figured. I liked him. So far. But I couldn't bear to be one of many.

Just then, a girl came bounding up to us, a damp T-shirt clinging to her breasts, long legs revealed in a short denim skirt. No bra. That was hard to miss.

She reached forward and wrapped her arms around Joel. He had a beer in one hand, the other hand hovering as if unsure what to do with it until he eventually placed it on her waist. She let go of him, also eventually.

I crossed my arms, barely able to watch, hoping this would all go away.

"Look at you," she said. "It's been so long."

"Hi, Charlotte," Joel said. "Um, lovely to see you."

I'd already seen rather too much of her when she'd been in the hot tub. I was sure she was one of the two girls. She tossed back her long blond hair, damp at the edges where she'd pinned it up earlier, touching Joel's arm as she spoke. And the woman could talk. She didn't stop with the talking and touching.

My stomach sank, not because Joel seemed taken with her, but because if there'd been a moment between Joel and me, it was gone. Besides, I'd been here before. There was always someone more attractive, more exciting, more 'something' than me.

I backed off a few steps, turned, and dragged myself back inside the house. Maybe I could catch up with Joel later when he wasn't so distracted.

Inside, I looked around for Nick and Lily. I knew a few people here, not many, and suddenly I needed my little sister like a security blanket. It wasn't like me at all. Had never been like me.

I wiped the perspiration from the back of my neck, but as I looked around no one else looked hot and bothered. Talking to Joel had done this to me, and nothing could be more ridiculous.

A drink was in order so I headed toward the bar in the corner. Didn't quite make it. Something strange caught my eye. If I wasn't mistaken, Lachie was lying on the sofa, his shirt off, a young woman on the floor in front of him with a tattoo gun in her hand. And on his chest.

I'd always been fascinated by tattoos. Not that I wanted one. It just wasn't 'me'. There was something so permanent about them, which was the whole point, I suppose. I liked changing things around all the time, like my hair, dyed a different color every few months. I hated to think what would happen if I got a tattoo and then decided I wanted a different one.

Though I hadn't spoken to her, I knew about Jess, Lachie's bodyguard, hanging around nearby frowning as she watched the tattoo in progress. Maybe this didn't fall within her job description.

I took a small step back. Bumped into something. *Someone.*

"You abandoned me." The words were whispered in my ear, a shiver shooting up my spine because I knew the voice.

I turned around slowly, looked up at Joel. So tall. At least four inches taller than me, and I was five feet ten.

No backing down, not for me. "I didn't abandon you."

"Oh, yes you did."

He was right. I had.

"You look like a champagne girl. Am I right?"

He handed me a flute, stepping back to give me some space.

I took a sip, felt the bubbles slide down my throat. "Ah, nothing tastes as good as free champagne."

"Yep, couldn't have said it better myself."

I shrugged. "Anyway, that's a no-brainer. All girls like champagne. Or nearly all of them."

"I could say the same about guys and beer."

"I guess so. Am I forgiven for the abandonment?"

"Of course. Nothing is too much trouble for a fan of Black Paisley."

He smiled, his eyes crinkling at the corners, his sparkling teeth nearly as dazzling as his eyes. My breath caught in my throat. If only I was a better judge of character. If only I could be more trusting.

I sipped my champagne, peering over the top of the flute. "Oh, I didn't say I *liked* the band."

He feigned disappointment and I smiled right back at him, enjoying his company and the moment. Sometimes the moment was all you had.

His eyes on Lachie and the tattoo artist, Joel nudged

me. "Are you next?"

"No way!" I covered my mouth. "Not that there's anything wrong with tattoos. How about you? Are you covered in ink?"

He shook his head. "Never saw the need."

"Well, that's not very rock 'n' roll." I gave him my best admonishing look.

"Maybe that's where I went wrong. I need some tattoos, more piercings, maybe an addiction problem. And beautiful women hanging off me. All the rock stars have those." He linked his arm into mine, drawing me closer.

"You mean like groupies?"

"I wouldn't know about that."

He let me slip from his grasp. I'd liked the gentleness of his touch. I might even like it if he found some other excuse to touch me or take my hand.

"So Black Paisley doesn't have an entourage?" I asked.

"Ha! Not likely."

"So what do you do when you're not gigging?"

"You mean for a living? I'm a graphic designer."

"Really?"

"Yeah, I work at Chemistry Design."

"You're kidding. That's just around the corner from where I work. I walk past there nearly every day. I can't believe I haven't bumped into you."

I told him about my job at Intricate Interiors but my eyes were on Lily, making her way toward me. I waved for her to come over because she was my sister. Also because I loved her. And that was despite the fact I'd hoped to keep Joel all to myself a little longer.

I pulled her closer. "Joel, this is my sister, Lily."

He shook her hand, looked at me, raised his eyebrows.

"Your sister? You know, I would've guessed. That's some family resemblance."

"Most people can't see it," Lily said.

I nodded. We shared a house so I saw her every day but never got of sick of her. Or of Thomas, the world's cutest four-year-old. The thought of him sent a pang through my heart. I was going to miss them so much but I had to move out of their place sooner rather than later, the deadline of Lily's wedding looming.

"Well, it looks like there were enough good looks to get shared around your family," Joel said.

I hoped so. Lily laughed.

Joel frowned at my sister. "You look kind of familiar."

"I've lived here all my life," she said.

And she was about to be married to The Merchants' singer so her photo had been posted online and probably in magazines, even though they weren't the kind of publications I looked at. Hopefully Joel didn't look at them either.

"So have I," he said. "Maybe I've seen you around or at gigs."

"You know what Frankston is like," I said. "Everyone knows everyone else. Or at the very least there's that six degrees of separation thing."

"Especially if you play in a band," Lily added. "If you know Lachie, you must know Nick too." Her lips curled to a smile as she looked over my shoulder. "Speak of the devil."

Nick slid closer, kissed her on the mouth as she turned to face him. "There you are."

"Of course I'm here." Her smile broadened, her face lighting up. "Where else would I be?"

Maybe I should have kept Joel to myself a bit longer instead of talking to Lily. And now Nick was here, that made it a crowd.

I should introduce them. I should do Joel that small favor.

I reached for Nick's arm. "This is Joel. He plays in Black Paisley. They're a seriously good band. If you haven't seen them, you should check them out."

"I don't know if you remember us," Joel said. "You were in the audience once."

"Of course I remember," he said. "Your singer likes to jump around onstage a lot."

Joel nodded. "Yep, that was us."

I leaned closer to Nick. "Joel's a bass player."

"Yeah, I know. I've seen the band."

"And you're looking for a bass player," I added. "Joel has already said he'd love to play bass in The Merchants. In case you'd like to know."

"Um, thanks," Nick mumbled.

The color drained from Joel's face.

"I thought I should put it out there…" My voice trailed off.

"I think we've found someone already," Nick said.

He hadn't said anything about that or, if he had, it didn't ring a bell with me.

"That's my sister, always so direct," Lily blurted out before being distracted by her phone.

"Yeah, that's Scarlett." Nick put his arm around me, gave my shoulder a quick squeeze. He knew me all too well because I'd been blunt with him often enough in the past when I'd told him to take good care of Lily.

Judging by the look on Joel's face, he didn't know me

so well. Maybe I should have left my big mouth shut because this wasn't working out the way I planned. And now I didn't even know what I hoped or what I'd been thinking.

Her phone gripped in one hand, Lily touched Nick's arm and spoke to him softly while Joel and I stood in what could only be described as uncomfortable silence.

I leaned closer to Lily. "What's up?"

"That was Mom," she said. "Thomas has a fever."

"Is he okay?"

She nodded. "Mom gave him something for it and he's asleep again, but it's not fair to leave her with a sick child. Not fair to Thomas either. So I'm heading home. I told Nick he should stay."

Since I lived with them, I was used to the occasional fever or stuffy nose or vomiting episode. If it was something serious, Lily would have told me.

Still, somehow I wasn't in a partying mood anymore.

"I'll get my purse," Lily said.

She wandered off, Nick at her side.

Joel glared at me. "Why'd you do that?"

"Do what?"

"It was good getting an introduction but I'd been planning on breaking the news to Nick rather more gently."

"But you'd already mentioned it to Lachie. You told me so."

"Doesn't mean I wanted to blow things a second time after screwing up with him first. I looked like a dick back there."

I let that sink in. "So I blew it for you with Nick? I made you look like a dick?" He didn't answer, so I added,

"Sometimes it's better to get straight to the point. Then everyone knows where they stand."

"Yep, I guess so."

That wasn't what his face said. His lips were thin, no killer smile, no more sparkling eyes.

I didn't want to hang around where I wasn't wanted. I'd finally met a cute guy, an interesting guy, someone who was creative and got out there and followed his passion.

Meanwhile I'd ruined his chances of playing with The Merchants. And he probably didn't want to talk to me anymore either.

"Nice meeting you, Joel."

I turned but he grabbed my arm. "You're leaving?"

"Sure am."

I decided I'd rather keep my sister company and leave while the going was good. So I did.

Only the going wasn't good. Nowhere near it.

CHAPTER THREE

Joel

A few weeks had passed since I'd first met Nick and Lachie at his place, and now I was trying a different tactic—as barfly at The Swamp—probably the only barfly who stopped at one drink, but that was me.

Everyone knew The Swamp was Nick's bar, so that was exactly why I was here on a Thursday for lunch, leaning against the bar, scanning the room, trying to look casual.

I'd been taking every opportunity to talk to Nick whenever I saw him, and now we were practically best friends. Well, not quite. I'd ask him about the band, about Lily and their boy. About Scarlett too. I wanted to find out a lot more about her.

Tara, the manager, held my gaze when I turned back to the bar, one hand on her hip, the other resting on a beer tap. Yep, I was even on first name terms with the staff.

"The usual?" she asked.

I'd drunk water with my meal and had been hanging out for this. "You know me too well."

"Honey, I don't know you at all. I only know about

pouring beer." She smiled as she handed me an IPA with a magnificent foamy head.

I took a long sip. "That's good. One beer, then I've got to get back to work."

"You might want to hang around for a bit." She shifted her gaze to look behind me. I glanced over my shoulder to see Nick making his way inside, heading straight for the bar.

Turning back to Tara, I said, "You truly are a mind reader."

She shrugged. "I try."

I always had the feeling she was one of those people who knew more than they let on. She was also dating The Merchants' ex-bass player, and I was extremely grateful he was an *ex* because that left a space I might fill. I hadn't given up hope, couldn't give up, couldn't bear the thought.

Nick staggered to the bar. Not drunk, something else.

"What can I get you?" Tara asked.

He put a hand out. "I need a beer more than I've ever needed one in my life."

She frowned. "What's up?"

"I'm exhausted. I don't know how you women do it. All this organizing and shopping and wedding stuff is killing me. How can Lily spend so long looking at floral arrangements? They're flowers. They look pretty. End of story."

Tara shook her head. "You don't understand how women work."

"No, I don't."

I let out a nervous laugh. The desperation in Nick's eyes matched the despair I felt on the inside, anguish of a different kind because, despite my best efforts, any chance at getting an audition with The Merchants seemed to be slipping through my fingers.

"I don't know what you think is so funny," he said. "This could be you one day."

Smiling, I shook my head.

"I've gotta go." Nick clutched his beer like his life depended on it. "We're done with all that shopping so now I can finally sit down." To Tara. "Can you please bring some mineral water over for the girls?"

The girls? Was that what he'd said? I didn't dare turn around too quickly, so I waited a moment until Nick was leaving.

Scarlett and Lily stood inside the door, pointing and pondering over which table to take, when Scarlett spotted me. Surprise in her eyes. And a smile on her lips.

Another red outfit, another high neckline, her arms bared, the dress clinging to that waist, those hips, those boobs. Man, I should stop staring. And salivating.

It wasn't as though I hadn't thought about her. I had. I'd kept an eye out for her every time I left the office because I knew she worked nearby, disappointed every time because I'd never even caught a glimpse.

And now here she was. Desperation of a different kind flooded me.

Lily waved for Nick to join them, then made a beeline for a free table. Scarlett looked my way. Deliberated. Then went over to her sister and said something to her.

I held my breath. *Please let her come over.*

The two of them kept talking. Scarlett glanced my way. *Please.*

She turned and left her sister, heading right toward me while Nick passed her in the other direction, like two plates of my world shifting.

Seconds later, she sidled up beside me. Maybe not sidled, but I couldn't deny the closeness.

"Hi, Scarlett."

"I thought I should say hello, you know, since I blew things for you with Nick a few weeks back."

I shook my head. "You didn't blow it."

She smiled. "That's not what you said at the time."

"Maybe we can forget about that and start over."

"Sure." She glanced around the room. "So, do you come here often? Or is that line way too corny for you?"

"Corny is good." I nodded. "I like corny. And I like my dive bars too."

Her eyebrows lifted. "You like this place?"

"Yeah, I do. They've still got a band room, for one thing. A lot of places don't anymore."

She grimaced. "I'm glad it fits your grunge sensibilities, but The Swamp doesn't do it for me. I mean, look at the floor. What a mess."

"Hey, I like the crappy black and white checkered tiles. And the rips in the vinyl on the barstools. It adds character."

"You're not going to tell me you like the ceiling?"

Years ago, someone had painted the ceiling beams black and stuck old newspapers between them. A masterpiece in my opinion.

I shrugged. "I think they did a great job with the ceiling. It finishes the place off."

She held a hand out. "Well, I'm a bit of a neat freak and I have sensibilities. Interior architecture and design sensibilities, and this place breaks every rule."

"Maybe that's why I like it."

"You're allowed to like it. I don't mind if you're wrong." A smile tugged at those lush lips. "Anyway, you must know Nick is renovating. They're closing down soon so they can give the place an overhaul."

"Yeah, I heard. Did you have anything to do with that? I mean, you're an interior architect after all."

"No, Austin is his architect. Has been from the get-go."

Which was what I'd thought because I'd seen the ex-bass player here once or twice before, always deep in discussion with Nick so I'd never interrupted.

"Anyway, we're busy at my work," she said. "Not just at the moment, all the time, and I don't want to spend my weekends working on other jobs."

"Fair enough. But you're not at work today?"

"No, I took the day off to do some things with Lily."

"I heard."

"Really?" She raised her eyebrows. "Anyway, why don't you come and join us? If you think free beer is good, wait till you find out how good a free meal is going to taste."

My mouth was watering for reasons that had nothing to do with food and everything to do with hunger of a different sort. I'd love to have tasted everything on offer, but somehow doubted that was what she was suggesting.

"Actually, I've already eaten but I'd love to join you."

Placing my hand on her lower back, I ushered her ahead. Walking slowly, she turned, a sultry smile on her face, or maybe she couldn't help but look any other way. This felt like the beginning of something beautiful. Please, please let it be the beginning.

As we wove our way through the tables, I reached for

her hand. Any excuse. She felt warm and womanly.

"Hang on a sec," I said. "I need to have a quick word with my friends first."

I'd come here with people from work, and it felt rude to just dump them, so I took a few steps to their table and tapped George on the shoulder.

I leaned closer. "I'm just going to join some other friends at their table."

"No problem." George glanced back, spotting Nick. "Now you're mixing with the big guns."

He was a strange one. George would kill for my job as head of the design team. Meanwhile I'd kill for the chance to join The Merchants.

Scarlett reached for my arm and practically dragged me across to their table. "I brought a little friend with me."

Lily laughed. "Yep, tiny!"

I leaned over to shake her hand. "We've met before. I'm Joel."

"Yes, I remember. Don't mind me, I'm not getting up." She smiled. "You'll only made me look short."

"Have a seat." Nick put down the menu in his hand. "We were about to order, so you're just in time."

I held Scarlett's chair out for her and the two of us sat down. Side by side, just the way I liked it.

"I've already eaten, thanks," I said. "But I'd love to join you."

Nick nodded. "No problem. So are you here on your own?"

"No, I came with some colleagues."

Nick raised his eyebrows. "Colleagues? You mean you have a job?"

"Are you kidding me, Nick? Of course I have a job.

I'm a graphic designer." I pointed to the table on the other side of the room. "And those are the guys I work with."

"It's just..." He hesitated. "I've only ever seen you here on your own."

"Well, it'd be nice if I could make a living out of Black Paisley but that ain't happening. We've got a gig on Saturday night at Malone's, though. The guys would love it if you came along."

And I would absolutely love for Nick Steel to see me play again. He nodded, didn't say anything.

I turned to Scarlett because she was just as important as Nick, maybe more so. "I'd really like it if you came too."

She shrugged one pretty shoulder. "Sure."

Nick took Lily's hand into his. "Sometimes I'd rather stay home with the family."

He leaned closer to his fiancée and whispered something to her, both of them smiling. All of this relationship-bliss was absolutely not working in my favor. Couldn't he go out just for one night? Then maybe he could see if he liked the way I played bass.

"They're so damn happy together." Scarlett had a starry look in her eyes. "I mean, just look at them."

"Yep, you got that right."

She tilted her head. "Doesn't leave much room for me, though."

"How do you mean?"

Her shoulders slumped. "I live with them."

"What? Like in the spare room?"

"I know that might seem weird, but it's kind of the way things ended up. Nick and Lily broke up years ago and only got back together recently, but Nick has always taken care of Lily and Thomas. He bought a house for them even if he didn't live there. Whereas I did. I live there."

"So you've always shared a house with them?"

"Not quite. Until about a year ago, I was in a long-term relationship, living with a guy, thinking I was pretty damn happy myself. Then we broke up." The hitch in her voice told me this was still painful for her.

"It happens." I'd had enough breakups in my time too, mostly because I'd been in lots of relationships. Not all of them deep, mind you. Very few, in fact.

"I needed a place to stay so I moved in with Lily and Thomas." Her eyes lit up. "I absolutely adore Thomas, and Lily and I get along so well."

If she was used to living with a small child, maybe she was used to chaotic conditions. Maybe we could work something out.

As I stared into Scarlett's warm brown eyes, an idea came to mind. Not a silly idea, a practical one, something that might fit both our needs.

"What about you?" she asked. "What's your family like?"

"The usual, two parents, a younger brother." Scarlett looked at me expectantly so I added, "My mom's Indian, Dad's a white guy, and my brother and I are somewhere in between. We're a close family, probably because it's just the four of us and Grandma here in Nevada."

Except I'd always felt different from the rest of the family. Since Grandpa had died anyway. Somehow that old guilt kept surfacing.

In a few days, the others were going on vacation to India—Grandma, Mom, Dad, Alex and his fiancée—but I hadn't wanted to go in the first place. I'd never felt particularly Indian. I'd only ever felt like me.

Then I'd backed out of the trip when I found out about The Merchants. My dreams meant too much to me.

Scarlett nodded. "I'd wondered about your background."

This wasn't the subject I wanted to talk about. "Can we get back to you? Are you planning on moving out?"

Her shoulders slumped. "Yeah, I've been looking for a while. Ideally I'd prefer to share a place because I like some company when I come home from work, but if I can't find anything I'll have to find a one-bedroom place and live on my own." She shrugged. "I'm sure I'd get used to it."

I hadn't been in a hurry to find a new roommate since Dave moved out. He'd only been gone a couple of weeks. Suddenly I felt the sense of urgency increasing.

"You can stay with me."

Scarlett's eyes widened. I could hardly believe the words coming from my mouth either.

"I've got a spare room," I said. "Dave, my old roommate, moved out to live with his girlfriend so his room is free. I've been asking around to see if I could find someone to move in. I've been putting off advertising the room. You get a lot of weirdos that way. But that'd be the next step. Unless you're interested."

Could I even share a house with a woman? I'd lived with Mia many years ago, but living with a girlfriend was way different from having a roommate. And all my roomies had been guys. My pulse racing, I tried to keep my cool.

"Hmm," Scarlett murmured.

I spread my arms. "Two birds with one stone, that's all I'm saying. I've got a room and you're looking for one. It'd be a help to me too, what with a mortgage and all."

"So it's your place? You own it?"

"Yep, me and the bank, but that's usually the way."

I nodded, tried not to look too enthusiastic or desperate. Truth was, I could cover the mortgage without the extra rent, even if the money would make my life easier. It was Scarlett I needed desperately and that made this a whole different ballgame.

Her brow knotted in thought. "Where is your place exactly?"

"Sawyer Hills."

"That's not far from where I am now. What's it like?"

"Fairly modest. Three bedrooms. A small yard."

And a lot of mess, the part I couldn't say. A hell of a lot of mess. I cringed. I hadn't cleaned the house in weeks. I spent so much time at work lately and I'd been completely consumed by this band thing and trying to catch up with Nick. And I had to admit, I'd probably been more of a slob since Dave moved out.

"Maybe I could take a look around," she said.

"Sure."

"What about straight after lunch?"

Panic shot through me. No way could I show her the place in its current state. She'd run a mile.

I shook my head. "I have to get back to work."

"What time do you finish? I could come by later on today."

"Sure."

I nodded, seemingly calm on the outside, while I tried to work out how I was going to get the place into a decent state when I'd have to rush home from work to do the world's fastest cleaning.

"No problem," I added.
Not much.

CHAPTER FOUR

Scarlett

What was I getting myself into? Only one way to find out.

I pulled up outside Joel's house. It was an older neighborhood with tree-lined streets, much like my current place. Not much traffic. As I got out of the car, the only sounds were those of children playing ball further down the street, something that made me feel at home right away.

The yards of nearby houses were well tended and looked cared for, which was more than I could say about Joel's place. Clearly, he wasn't into mowing the lawn.

A woman looked up from next door where she was bent over her roses, so I smiled at her.

"Hello," she called out.

I wandered closer. "Hi."

"If you're looking for Joel, he's home. I heard him in the backyard earlier."

"Actually, I might be looking to move in." I waited to see if she had a reaction, only a smile. "So I'm taking a look around first."

"Joel's a heck of a nice guy, but you probably already

know that. Are you a musician too?"

"You've heard him play?"

"My kids like dancing along to the music." She waved it off. "Never late at night, though. He's very considerate."

"Great, thanks."

"Catch you later."

I wandered up the front path. She clearly liked Joel. That had to be a good thing. In fact, the simple act of a neighbor saying hello was a good thing.

I knocked on the door, heard a door banging in the distance, then the thump of footsteps on floorboards before the door was pulled open.

Joel's hair hung over his face until he shook it back to reveal his wide dark eyes. "You're early."

"No, I don't think so."

"I, ah, might be running a bit late."

If he wanted me to come back later, that wasn't happening. I smiled and he pulled the door open further so I could step inside.

"Nice polished floorboards," I said.

"Come in."

He ushered me into the living room. It was probably just as well he was standing behind me so he couldn't see the shock on my face.

A large front window looked out onto the street, and if anyone were looking inside, they'd see wall-to-wall mess. There was furniture and there was floor, most of it covered with old newspapers, pieces of clothing, and miscellaneous bits of scrunched up paper.

"Wow." That was better than a lot of the other words that could have escaped my lips.

Joel came forward, ran a hand through his hair. "I'm

sorry about the state of the place. I got stuck at work and didn't get a chance to clean up properly."

"You've never cleaned up!"

"What do you mean?"

"Maybe it's better I don't say what I mean," I muttered as I made my way through the room. Carefully, because that was the only way.

A low sideboard caught my eye. Mid-century in design it looked like it could have come from the set of Mad Men.

"Such a beautiful piece." I ran my fingers along the top, accidentally knocking over a pile of magazines. "I'm sorry."

A wooden box carved with elephants sat beneath the magazines, a strange item to say the least.

"I should put that in a safe place," Joel said. "I use it to store some old Indian jewelry my mom gave me."

I turned away, surveying the room. As much as I liked Joel, this room said a lot of things about him and none of them were good. Maybe this wasn't such a good idea after all.

But I had to find a place. I'd already left it too long, probably because I felt way too much at home where I was. Nick and Lily were getting married in a few weeks, and that was my personal deadline, even though I could possibly push it out another couple of weeks while they were away on their honeymoon.

And tomorrow I had to go back to work. Margaret had been all over the place lately, dumping more work on me so she could take long lunches. Then there was her sleazy husband who seemed to think a twenty-six-year-old like me might be interested in him. Better I didn't think about him.

"I met your neighbor," I said.

His eyes darkened. "Not Miss Henson?"

I held his gaze, unsure of the answer. "The lady next door. She said her kids liked your music."

He relaxed. "Just as well you didn't talk to the neighbor on the other side. She complains about everything. Apparently, last spring, the birds in the oak tree out the back were too noisy for her. She told me I should get the tree chopped down."

"You didn't, did you?"

"Absolutely not."

"Can we continue the tour?" I asked, not certain I wanted the answer, not even sure I wanted to see the rest of the place, not sure of anything anymore.

"Sure." He motioned for me to follow. "I'm sorry it's such a mess. I'm not normally this bad."

"I find that hard to believe," I muttered.

He stopped in the kitchen. "See, I've started cleaning up in here."

And he had. It gave me hope. The countertops had been wiped clean, the sink gleaming, and if I wasn't mistaken, he'd even mopped the floor. It had the same black and white checkered tiles as The Swamp, only these were in good condition.

The window had a lovely outlook to the backyard. The oak he'd mentioned looked magnificent, not something you'd ever want to chop down.

A shed at the rear of the yard caught my eye. Painted in a pretty red, it could have been pulled from a yard in New England or even Norway. Double doors with oversized black hinges, crisp white window frames, and faux shutters painted black to match the shingles made it look like a hideaway.

I stepped toward the door at the side of the room. "Is it okay if I have a look outside?"

"But you can see through the kitchen window." He pulled the curtains aside. "See."

"Just a quick look, that's all."

Panic in his face. "Um, you can't. The door's locked."

My hand on the doorknob, I turned it gently, couldn't help myself. "No, it's not."

Joel clapped a hand to his mouth, the look on his face telling me he wasn't going to stand in my way.

Pulling the door open, I stepped onto the threshold and it all became evident. He'd scooped up all the trash from the kitchen and maybe some from the living room, tossing it out of sight, ready to dispose of later. 'Later' hadn't come. I'd got here too soon. Meanwhile the trash was blocking the side path so I had no chance of making my way to the yard.

"I was cleaning up," he said meekly.

"No kidding."

I closed the door. Pressed a hand to my temple. "I'm having a bit of trouble with this. So the place was worse before you got home?"

He nodded. "I'm a bit of a slob, I admit, but I can change. After Dave left, I felt like I didn't need to bother so much anymore. I let the place go. Maybe it's kind of a guy thing."

I threw my hands up. "Next thing you know you'll be telling me your mom does your washing for you."

"She wanted to, but I wouldn't let her." He hung his head, which made me laugh, then added, "Give me a chance. That's all I'm saying. Let me show you the spare room. Your room."

Taking my hand, he made me feel secure even though that wasn't the case. Damn it, he'd made such a good impression that I couldn't reconcile the state of his house with the gorgeous guy I'd met.

At the end of the hall, he pulled open a door and we stepped inside. Light streamed in through French doors that looked out onto the red shed at the back of the yard. Sunflower yellow walls brightened the room even further, while cornflower blue cornices and skirting boards framed the room, the colors contrasting beautifully. Sunflowers and cornflowers. Not a color scheme I would have chosen but it was so refreshing and honest that it filled me with warmth.

"I can help you repaint the room if you don't like it," Joel said.

"I don't like it. I *love* it." One thing seemed strange. "And this was Dave's room? He painted it these colors?"

"Yeah."

I frowned. "Was he gay?"

"No, nothing like that. He's a designer and he's into his color."

I nodded, taking in the ambiance, the sense of space. "This is enormous."

"The best room in the house."

"So why'd you let Dave have the biggest and best room?"

"I've got a bedroom and then the spare room is for my music gear and my art stuff."

"Art stuff?"

"I do a bit of painting and drawing. Anyway, it only seemed fair that Dave got the biggest room."

How generous.

I looked around. If I placed my bed against the wall opposite the French doors, I could sit up in bed in the morning and look out on the yard. I had a pair of 1950s freestanding closets that'd fit perfectly along one wall. I could even set up a reading nook or study area in the corner with plenty of space to spare. Unlike my current room, I'd have room for my yoga mat. Hell, I could probably run a whole yoga class in here.

I stopped myself. I was moving in mentally already. What was I thinking?

My head was spinning. Maybe I should go with my gut. After all, what was the worst thing that could happen? I'd hate the arrangement and then have to move into a small apartment on my own. That was already my Plan B. I wouldn't be any worse off.

"What do you think?" Joel asked.

"It's a beautiful room."

"The rest of the house is a mess, I know. You caught me unprepared, that's all. If you come back tomorrow, everything will be different, you'll see. And by the weekend it'll be spotless."

"You think you can do 'spotless'?"

"Absolutely."

I was heading closer to a 'yes' every minute. This wouldn't be anything like living with Ronan because this was a completely different set of circumstances and Joel wasn't my boyfriend. I wouldn't be depending on him for honesty or faith. Or fidelity.

A pang cutting through my heart, I forced myself to think about the subject at hand.

If I was absolutely desperate, Nick had already said I

could move into his old apartment. He was still using the music room, the living room too because he'd spread himself out, and hadn't yet started building a new studio at the back of Lily's place. Still, I knew that wasn't the place for me.

"I'm pretty easygoing most of the time," Joel said. "Not so hard to live with. I'll do my own thing and you do yours. Friends can do that. And as a friend, I'm still hoping you'll come to the gig at Malone's on Saturday night, regardless of whether you move in or not."

A gig, not a date. My head was moving too fast or maybe that was my heart. Either way I had to get a grip. I did like the band, after all. And I could help him out too because there was a slim chance I may have been too brusque when I'd introduced him to Nick the first time we'd met.

"I'll see if I can convince Nick to come too," I said. "You'd like that, wouldn't you?"

He nodded, his dark eyes widening. "I was going to ask about that. Not that Nick is the reason I'd like you to come along. I just figure it's better to be up front about this stuff."

"I couldn't agree more."

Joel wasn't like Ronan, not at all. In fact, I should stop thinking about my ex and start thinking about what I wanted.

"If you're considering moving here on the weekend and you need a hand, I can borrow a friend's van," Joel said.

I asked him how much he was charging for the room. A very reasonable amount as it turned out.

"Okay, you've got a deal."

I came out with it before I changed my mind. Joel grinned, his eyes crinkling at the corners as he pushed his hair behind his ears. This guy was way too good looking and that was throwing me. I shouldn't let myself get taken in by it.

Except maybe I already had.

CHAPTER FIVE

Joel

We'd already set up our equipment on stage, the drum kit, our amps and instruments, leaving this area pretty much empty except for a table, a couple of crappy chairs, and the obligatory milk crates that seemed to be backstage at every venue I'd ever played.

Head down, I paced the floor, staring at the concrete floor.

I couldn't fucking believe it. Of all the nights Jay had chosen to screw up, he had to do it tonight. This wasn't the first time but at least the other times he hadn't been completely off his face. He'd still been able to get up there and sing.

Not tonight, though, the one time Nick and Scarlett were going to be in the audience.

"Fuck," Brian said.

He was slouched on his drum stool while Tim sat on a table jammed in the corner, shoulders slumped.

"You got that right," I said.

While I'd been helping move Scarlett's furniture, mowing the lawn, and cleaning the house, the two guys had suspected something was wrong and had paid Jay a visit. He'd been flaked out on the sofa, so high his mind was in outer space, unable to speak let alone stand. No way could he get up on stage with us even if we propped him up and taped a microphone to his hand.

Meanwhile his dumb-ass druggie girlfriend had told the guys they should get the hell out and mind their own business—'their own fucking business' to be more precise.

I raked a hand through my hair. Couldn't stand it any longer so I kicked a couple of milk crates over, an empty beer can skittering on the concrete while the crates toppled.

My phone vibrated. Scarlett's name flashed on the screen with a short message:

Is everything ok?

"I'll be back in a sec, guys," I said.

When we'd first started the band, I'd told Brian and Tim that Jay was an addict, that his problem was much bigger than he was letting on, but they'd let it slide. I always suspected they thought it was cool or a part of the lifestyle or maybe they'd truly believed he was only dabbling. As far as I was concerned, this wasn't rock 'n' roll. It was bullshit.

I took a deep breath as I went out the door into the main bar. I shouldn't take this out on Brian and Tim, and didn't want to take it out on Scarlett. I so badly wanted to make things right with her, to show her how good the band was, to bring her into my life.

My heart lifted at the sight of her waving from the other end of the bar. In a room full of people Scarlett was a beacon. Not because of her short blond hair or her height, though that helped, but because of the way her personality shone in her face. Vibrant. Full of life.

She was also by herself, which I wasn't expecting.

I raised my eyebrows. "I thought Nick was coming?"

"He's running late."

"Sorry, I would never have left you on your own if I'd known."

She smiled. "I'm a big girl."

"You don't mind that the place is a dive?"

"Goes with the territory. At least it's a step up from The Swamp."

Wood paneling made the room feel warmer and the brass fittings on the bar gave it a touch of class even if the timber was chipped and the brass tarnished. The sign above the bar was a big giveaway. *Shut up and drink*. You had to have a sense of humor to come here.

I'd already filled Scarlett in about Jay, told her we weren't sure what we were going to do.

I nodded toward the rear room. "You should join us, but I gotta warn you, the mood is not good back there."

"The mood is plenty good out here." She sipped the white wine I'd given her earlier. "This place is buzzing."

Which only made things worse. My gut twisted. All these people had come out tonight to see us, and we were going to let them down. We could cancel and give them their money back, a possibility we'd discussed but we had another plan, one that relied on me. My mouth went suddenly dry.

Scarlett frowned. "Sorry, have I said the wrong thing?"

"Not at all." I took her hand. "I'll introduce you to the guys."

We wove our way through the crowd. I pushed open the door to the backstage area, still wishing a miracle might happen and Jay would be standing there apologizing, somehow sober and coherent. No such luck.

The guys stood as I made the introductions and even managed to smile, which was truly something under the circumstances.

Tim looked across at Scarlett. "Don't suppose you can sing, can you?"

She placed a hand on her chest. "Me? The only song I can sing is *Happy Birthday*, and even that's not good."

He looked away. "I'm not so great either."

I steeled myself. "Brian, I'm going to need a hand."

His eyes widened. "Hang on. You're not saying…"

I held a hand out. "Take it easy. We can do this. It's only for one night. Doesn't have to be the end of the world."

Even if it felt like it was. The words I didn't say.

"You've got to be kidding me," Brian said. "Jay is totally wasted. We don't have a singer. Doesn't get much worse than this."

"We already talked about it. We'll ditch a few songs and I'll sing the rest. They're *my* songs. And I'm not going to let that stupid prick, Jay, ruin everything."

I ignored the fact that I wasn't front man material, also the minor problem that fucking up in front of a sizeable crowd was a distinct possibility.

I swallowed back the fear, refused to let it take over. "I need your help for a couple of songs, *Oblivion* and *Come to Me*. You're so good on the backing vocals. We'll switch it over so you're singing the lead and I'll do the backing. To give me a break for a bit. I'm going to need it."

Tim nudged him. "You can do it, Brian."

He hung his head. "I don't know about that."

"Don't you get it?" Tim became louder. "You *have* to do it. Besides, you're hiding behind a huge drum kit. What've you got to worry about?"

"Okay, okay. It might work."

I turned to Scarlett, noticed she'd taken a step back to give us room. I should've been paying her more attention. The night was turning to shit and we'd barely got started yet.

"Sorry to dump you in the middle of all this," I said.

She shook her head. "Not at all. Tell you what, I'll get you and the guys some beers."

What a gem. I should be doing the gig for Nick, for myself—and I was—but I wanted the band to rock tonight for Scarlett too. For her, above all, even if that didn't make sense.

"Tell the bartender you're with the band," I said. "They'll take it out of our tab. Same with your drinks."

"Bring back a whole case!" Brian yelled.

It broke the ice. The three of us laughed, and Scarlett shot us a smile over her shoulder as she left.

I grabbed a set list and crossed out the songs we were cutting out, then put an asterisk next to the two songs Brian would sing. Did the same on the other two set lists and scrunched up the fourth that was meant to be for Jay.

I handed Brian the page. "For you."

"Got it."

Then it hit me. What was I doing letting Scarlett go off for beers like she was our servant? I wasn't thinking, that was the problem.

"Be right back," I said to the boys.

As I strode back into the bar, Scarlett was struggling to get her hands around all the beers, not to mention the glass of white she was still drinking. Giving her my best smile, I swept the three beers from the counter.

"I'll come with you." Scarlett followed me backstage.

Tim and Brian hadn't moved. I didn't know if that was good or bad. This was hard on them too, something I shouldn't forget.

"You guys deserve a beer." I handed them the long necks, then chugged back some beer myself. Dutch courage.

Scarlett reached for her phone, looked down, then back up at me. "Nick's on his way."

I'd told the guys he'd be here because I knew they'd be thrilled. Nothing like having one of your idols in the audience. That had been earlier, before the shit had hit the fan with Jay.

The guys didn't have as much riding on this as I did though, nowhere near it. Brian was moving to San Francisco with his girlfriend in a couple of months. Meanwhile Tim's wife was pregnant with twins and he was more than happy to forget about the band. Soon there'd be no more Black Paisley.

The bar manager pushed open the door. "Hey, guys, time to go on."

I nodded. "No problem."

Not much. He left, which was just as well because it was better he didn't notice the looks on our faces. I turned to the guys, motioning for them to get up.

They stood, Brian brushing some imaginary dirt from the front of his jeans, both of them dawdling. Couldn't say I blamed them.

Warm fingers intertwined with mine. Scarlett.

"Break a leg." Her smile was bright even in the dim

light. "Isn't that what they say?"

"That's for actors."

And I was going to have to be a damn good actor to get away with this tonight. My heart raced, perspiration beading on my brow.

Scarlett stood on tiptoes and placed the world's quickest kiss on my cheek. Friendly. Sweet. Still, it took my breath away.

I leaned closer, let her see it was coming and pressed a slow kiss to her cheek, stopped myself from taking her into my arms. How could I even be thinking of that at a time like this?

She was beaming, a glint in her eyes. "Good luck."

Turning away, she was gone in an instant. My heart stopped. I swear no female in the history of womankind had ever looked so good from behind. Long legs, the curve of her hips in that skirt, the dip of her waist, her pretty little shoulder as she looked over it and shot me a smile.

"Hey, are you ready or what?" Tim's voice.

"Y-yeah, sure."

My heart back in working order, the three of us strode onto the stage. I picked up my bass, plugged the lead in, played a few notes. Just the right amount of thump, enough top end to cut through, perfect.

Time to face the audience, except I could barely look at them. Brian had settled behind the drum kit, Tim eyeing me up from the other side of the stage as he strummed a chord.

Jay usually came up with some smartass introduction before we played. Shit, I should probably do that too but my throat was tight, nerves rising up from my stomach.

I wished I was somewhere else. Anywhere. Wished I was Travis Scott falling through the stage or Dave Grohl breaking a leg in the middle of a concert, then maybe this would all be over.

I nodded at Tim for him to begin and he launched into the first number. Glancing back at Brian, we joined in—drums and bass locked in together. We did our thing. The music took over, sunk into my chest, spread through my whole body. I could feel the music.

End of the song. Shit. I stared out at the crowd. Faces, dark. Applause. We'd done it.

I leaned in to the mic. "Thank you all for coming tonight." More clapping, I couldn't believe it. It spurred me on. "Jay couldn't make it this evening but you're still stuck with the three of us, so tonight we're gonna have to be extra loud."

The next song opened with bass so I charged across the stage as I played, put on a performance, egging Tim on, and watching him throw himself into it. I only just made it back to my mic in time for the vocals. And I sang my guts out.

I could do this. *We* could do this. It was hard to make out faces with the lights in our eyes but Scarlett was doing her beacon thing, standing to one side at the front with Nick beside her.

Brian belted out his two numbers as planned, gave me a break, the chance to re-energize. I kept up the between-songs-patter because the audience deserved to be talked to and, hey, I wasn't so bad at this.

Time to slow things down a little.

"How many of you..." I scanned the audience, caught Scarlett's eye. "How many of you remember what it felt like the first time you fell in love? Or had your heart broken? Do you remember that? This song is for you."

A couple of girls at the front swooned, actually swooned. I wanted to move people, make them feel something, give them songs they enjoyed.

The opening chords were quiet, melodic. I leaned closer to the mic.

> *A beating heart*
> *Waiting to be split apart*
> *A frozen room*
> *That feeling of doom*
> *You're never gonna know how much this hurts*
> *You'll never feel my pain*

Guitar, bass, drums, building, driving, working together. A long moan, from me. Then I belted out the chorus.

> *My pain, my pain*
> *Don't say the words*
> *Don't let him in*
> *Say it's me, always me*

I looked into Scarlett's eyes. And I felt the pain, the emotion, the heartbreak. Lost in the melody and melancholy of the words, I let it all out, gave it every ounce of feeling.

To her, for Scarlett, everything.

Suddenly the song was over, the audience clapping, the girls at the front looking like they were about to wet their pants. And Scarlett shining.

"Goodnight, everybody," I said.

The crowd clapped, wouldn't stop cheering as Tim and I stepped back, ready to pack up our gear.

Yelling. *More, more.*

Shit, what to do. We only had one more song that was a possibility. I spoke to the guys. And we hit it one more time. Killed it, in fact.

Afterward, I held a hand out to the crowd. "Thank you. You've been a wonderful audience. Drive home safely and, if you're not driving, then drink as much as you like."

A giant cheer from the crowd. I wasn't even sure what happened next. I took my bass off. We ended up backstage. The guys couldn't stop grinning. Someone shoved a beer into my hand. Scarlett threw her arms around me for a hug. I warned her I'd be sweaty. Nick shook my hand. People gathered around. Friends. Friends of friends.

This was why I played. For the high and the way it made me feel. Well, one of the reasons, anyway. Because this moment and the wave I'd been riding on stage cancelled out all the shitty things that had come before and made it all worthwhile.

I pulled Scarlett closer. I should probably be speaking to Nick, trying to talk my way into The Merchants, but that could wait.

Her brown eyes widened. "You were amazing."

"I couldn't have done it without you."

A blush spread to her cheeks. "Don't be silly."

"It's true. When I sang *A Beating Heart*, that was for you. Couldn't you tell?"

Though not usually shy, her lips curved to a timid smile. I liked being the one who put a smile on her face. It filled me with warmth, made me feel comfortable, and something more.

I took a deep breath. I'd never sung a song for a girl like this, not with all my heart, and there'd been plenty of girls.

"Joel, my man." Nick shook my hand, then changed his mind and pulled me in for a one-armed hug. "You guys were on fire."

A grin took over my face. I couldn't help it when I was being complimented by one of my favorite musicians, especially now I had newfound respect for lead vocals and exactly how hard it was to be the front man.

"Thanks," I said. "It was hard work tonight, but worth it."

"Which of the songs are yours?"

I looked at him blankly. "Sorry?"

"Which songs did you write? Or do you write them together as a band?"

"All mine. I write the bass and guitar parts and the words, and then let Brian do his own thing on drums."

Nick nodded. "Impressive. You've got some cool lyrics too."

"We had a few issues tonight." I'd almost forgotten my anger at Jay. Almost. "Sorry about the, uh, execution."

"The execution was fuckin' great."

He sounded like he meant it. Nick Steel liked my execution. How good was that?

"You can play," he added.

I swallowed. "Thanks, I've been doing this for a while."

"Scarlett told me about what happened with your singer."

"Yeah, let's just sat there was a bit of a glitch."

I couldn't believe it. 'The glitch' staggered through the door into the backstage area. Jay could stand. Walk even. Only just. His eyes glazed, his skin sallow, he looked as out of it as anyone I'd ever seen.

"Are we ready, guys?" he yelled.

People stopped and stared, then ignored him and carried on with their conversations. Anger burned in gut, rising to my throat.

Nick frowned. "Hey, isn't that...?"

"Yeah, it is."

Nick's eyes widened. "And that's..."

Yep, look who was hanging off Jay. If it wasn't Domino, crazed eyes staring as if he was on another planet. I didn't know what he'd been taking but it wasn't good. This wasn't heroin chic. It was two pricks who thought they were rock stars.

Brian and Tim rushed across the room, the two of them towering over Jay.

"Lemme go on stage," he mumbled. "We gotta play."

Jay didn't stand a chance as the two of them pushed him out of the room, Domino stumbling along beside them, protesting about how they couldn't do that. Everyone stared. It was hard not to.

I pulled Scarlett closer. "Are you okay?"

"Sure."

Brian and Tim returned a few minutes later, receiving a high-five from a girl in the doorway. They marched toward us.

Tim shook his head. "Guy's got nerve."

"What about Domino?" Nick asked.

"What about him?"

Nick's lips went thin. "He told me he was on vacation until a week ago."

"It wasn't vacation." Tim spat the words out. "It was rehab. And it didn't work."

Not only that, he was sharing his gear with our singer.

Surely this couldn't be happening all over again. Okay, Domino hadn't exactly stolen Olivia from me all those years ago, but she'd left me for him. And for drugs. Because both those things were way more exciting than me. It still hurt.

Nick turned to me. "Do you want to have a jam with us next week?"

"What? I mean, yeah sure." I tried to keep my shit together.

"It's not an audition, not exactly." Nick shrugged. "Well, I have to talk to the other guys first."

"Uh, no problem."

Brian gave me a friendly punch on the shoulder while Tim looked equally surprised. Shocked would be more like it.

They made the most of the opportunity to chew the fat with Nick, and I couldn't blame them.

I was still in a state of shock myself as Scarlett jumped up and down on the spot and threw her arms around me.

"That's fantastic," she whispered in my ear.

I drew her closer, didn't want to let her go, but this wasn't the time or the place. I didn't know what the hell was going on anymore. My heart was racing, head spinning, in the best way possible.

She held me at arms' length, looked into my eyes, made me feel like a million dollars. "You were awesome on stage tonight. No wonder Nick's impressed."

"Nick's impressed?"

"He didn't say that exactly, but he is. You did it!"

"I couldn't have done it without you."

She shrugged. "I helped get Nick here tonight but that was all. The rest was up to you."

That wasn't all. She didn't get it. I'd been desperate to make a good impression on Nick tonight, but when I went on stage I wasn't playing for him.

It was for Scarlett. All for her.

CHAPTER SIX

Scarlett

Saturday night's gig was a hundred years ago, or two days ago, I wasn't sure which. Joel had helped me move the last of my stuff on Sunday and we'd spent the rest of the day cleaning and tidying, which was very domestic of us.

He'd been kind of jittery, still on a high after the gig, but down to earth at the same time. He'd be cleaning the bathroom and would come into my room, scrubbing brush still in hand, making some remark about the gig and how well it had gone. Then he'd go back to work, leaving me with a smile on my face.

Now Monday morning was hitting me like a slap to the face. I dreaded the thought of going back to the real world. I wanted to stay here all day, at Joel's place, which already felt like my place, at the breakfast table or even in another room.

He'd made pancakes. No blueberries, but I could live with that when there was plenty of maple syrup. Our plates were empty, coffee had been drunk, and it was time for reality to take over.

I let out a long sigh. "I'll do the cleaning up."

Joel reached for the plates as he stood. "No, I'll take care of it. This is my treat to you for the beginning of your first working week in your new place. To make you feel at home."

I rested my chin on my hand. "That's the last thing you need to worry about."

"Sorry?"

"Nothing." I should stop daydreaming and hop to it. "Thanks so much. I'll go and get ready for work."

I had applying morning makeup down to a fine art so I went through my routine of eyeliner and mascara, followed by a swipe of lip gloss. My hair took a bit more time, since I liked to use product to give it shape and keep it in place.

I washed my hands, then dried them, my eyes wandering to the empty shower recess with its sparkling white tiles. My mind wandered too. Joel had been in there this morning. He'd stood there, tall, lean and naked. He'd let the water and soap stream over his body. He must look amazing naked.

I draped the towel on the rail evenly, stopped myself from straightening Joel's towel, forced myself to stop thinking about him. We shared a house. That was all.

As I came out of the bathroom, Joel stopped at the other end of the hallway and called out to me.

"I'm off. Have a good day."

A leather satchel slung over his shoulder, he strode away, the house suddenly feeling quiet and empty.

I grabbed my keys and backpack, a Crumpler in a funky chrysanthemum pattern. This morning I was stopping to pick up samples from a stone supplier and a fabric agency on my way to work. That way, after I got to the studio I could spend the rest of the day at my desk concentrating on my computer drawings. It was why Margaret had hired me, or one of the reasons, because she'd never managed to get her head around the AutoCAD program.

The stone samples didn't take long because my usual contact wasn't at the showroom so he'd left the materials ready for me to pick up. The fabric samples took longer because their new textile range had just arrived and I took the opportunity to check them out.

I parked in my usual spot in the parking garage underneath the building and used the stairs. As I came out of the stairwell, I waved to the receptionist at the office on the other side of the landing.

And turned to see the lights were off in the studio, which was odd given it was already after ten. I dug into my backpack for the key, made my way inside, and opened the blinds. Margaret had chosen this place for the huge windows and also for the space even though there were only two of us.

Settling at my desk, I checked my phone first because Margaret would have texted if she was going to be late. Nope, no messages.

Maybe there'd be something in my emails. I skimmed through the list, then stopped in my tracks. The subject line simply said 'Sorry Darling'. From Margaret.

Dear Scarlett,

I'm so sorry to do this to you but there was no other way. By the time you read this I'll be in Buenos Aires with Diego. I've had enough. I'm finished with Rod and with the business. I'm not coming back.

I'm going off grid for a while so you won't be able to reach me.

Thank you for all your work and everything you've done. I couldn't have asked for a better employee. I'm sure you'll find another job soon. They'll be lucky to have you.

All the best,

Margaret

My mouth open and eyes wide, I read it a second time. Leaned back in my chair with a thump.

Was this a joke? Except Margaret didn't joke around. She hadn't said much to me about Diego, her tango teacher, but I'd noticed the long lunches she'd been taking, the way her face would light up when the phone rang, the general change in her mood. As far as I knew, she'd only taken up the tango a couple of months ago but, then, maybe I didn't know much.

This couldn't be happening. I needed a job, couldn't survive without one. It felt like a bad dream. As if I'd walked into someone else's life.

Hearing a clicking sound, I looked up. Margaret's husband fumbled with the door before stumbling in. His eyes bleary, hair mussed up, he'd tucked a collared shirt into his jeans, the fabric stretched over his large stomach. If I'd hoped Margaret's email was a weird hoax, the look on his face told me otherwise.

I pointed to my computer screen. "Is this for real?"

He rushed across the room, his hands on my shoulders as he leaned all over me, pressing himself against my back. I stiffened. This was why I couldn't stand the guy.

I gave him a moment to read the email, then rolled my chair to the rear, forcing him to back off so I could get up. I didn't need his hands on me, no matter what had happened. I moved away, leaning against Margaret's desk—her old desk—while he stood beside mine.

"Did she say anything to you?" He stared. "Did you know she was doing this?"

"No."

"Are you sure you weren't encouraging her with this ... this *Diego*?"

"I've never even met the guy."

"She had no right." His voice cracked.

As much as I didn't want to feel sorry for Rod, a pang of sympathy stabbed through me. Dumped for the tango teacher. Talk about tacky. Besides, I felt the same sense of injustice at being ditched without warning, without any consideration or thought.

His shoulders slumped, he leaned against my desk. "She cleaned out the joint bank account."

Margaret was the money in the relationship. She'd always told me that. So where did this leave me?

"Rod, I know this is a bad time but Margaret owes me money too. There's my salary and vacation—"

He looked away. "Not my problem."

My mouth fell open. "Sorry?"

"Intricate Interiors was her business. It has nothing to do with me."

I pressed a hand to my temple. I wasn't sure what to do about the clients who were depending on us, or the projects that were already underway. I'd have to work that out later. Meanwhile my pulse was racing, stomach clenched into a knot.

"Scarlett..." Rod's voice softened as he stepped closer. "This might not be the end of the world."

I held a hand out. "Stop right there."

He didn't, sidling up closer to stand inches away from

me. "We might still be able to salvage something from the situation. The two of us."

I glared. "There is no *two of us*, Rod."

"We could join forces, start a new business, take up from where Margaret left off. You could work for me. We'd be good together."

He had to be kidding. The man knew nothing about interior architecture or business and he sure as hell didn't know me because if he thought he was getting any closer than he already was, he was sorely mistaken.

I spun around to grab my backpack. "Just so there's no misunderstanding between us, let me say I don't want to work with you, Rod. I don't trust you and I'm getting out of here."

He edged forward.

"Lock up before you go," I yelled as I walked out the door.

I raced down the stairs, knowing it'd be quicker than the elevator, my lungs set to explode by the time I burst through the double doors onto the pavement. A hand on my chest, I took a few moments to compose myself as I tried to work out what to do. My car was in the parking garage but I wasn't stupid enough to go there alone, not while Rod was still in the building. I didn't even know where I was going.

Except I did.

In a daze, I ambled around the corner. I knew the route well, the same path I took every day to go to Mario's Espresso Bar, but coffee was not what I needed right now. No, I needed ... someone.

There it was, the building Joel worked in. I checked the directory, pressed the button for four, and got into the elevator.

Wandering up to the reception desk, I felt like an automaton, as if my brain and body had been set on automatic.

"Is Joel Hitchcock here please?" I asked.

The receptionist picked up her phone. "May I ask your name?"

"Scarlett Novak."

I wasn't paying attention as she spoke into the phone and then to me. I nodded politely, looked around. The huge open-plan space had been separated into work areas with a kitchen in full view to the right. Rough walls were painted white, light pouring in through large steel-framed windows, enormous girders lining the ceiling above.

Joel appeared, looked every bit as good as he had this morning. "Scarlett?"

I let my eyes wander around the room a little longer. "I should've known you'd work in a cool loft conversion."

"Well, this used to be a factory." He stepped closer. "What's going on? I wasn't expecting you."

"Me neither. I wasn't expecting any of this."

He frowned. "Scarlett, what's happened? Are you okay?"

"I just got fired."

Eyes wide. "You got fired?"

"I lost my job. No, I didn't exactly lose it. It ran away from me. My boss, Margaret, it was her. She ran away."

He took my hand into his. "We need to talk. Don't move, I'll be right back. I just need to tell the guys where I'm going. Then I'll buy you a coffee."

Maybe I did need coffee after all. I nodded, waited, then we wandered off together to Mario's, somewhere I felt comfortable.

Joel ordered coffees and sat me down in a booth where it felt like there was only the two of us.

I started explaining. He took my hand into his. I kept rambling. He squeezed my hand. He listened. And I became more coherent.

"Sorry for losing it before," I said. "I don't know what I was thinking. I dragged you away from work for this."

"I'm glad you did. You needed to talk." He smiled. "And I was the one who did the dragging."

Resting my chin on one hand, a wave of melancholy overcame me, despite the fact I tried to tell myself I'd been through worse. This wasn't personal. It wasn't anything like what had happened with Ronan.

My breath caught in my throat at the memory, the stabbing pain in my heart all too real. When we were breaking up he'd given me the old line about how it wasn't me, it was him, but I'd known there was someone else. Suddenly the pieces had fit together.

Eventually he'd admitted it. The ultimate betrayal. And heartbreak because despite everything, I'd loved him. I'd given him everything I had, the best of me, while he'd been giving himself to someone else.

So, in comparison, being dumped by my boss didn't compare. Still, I had to wonder if there was something about me that attracted untrustworthy people.

"I'm a practical person," I said. "I've always had a job, ever since high school. Things like this aren't supposed to happen. Look at me, I'm homeless and jobless."

Joel shook his head. "You're not homeless. Don't worry about the rent if that's what's bugging you. It can wait till you get back on your feet again."

"I couldn't let you do that. It's very generous, too generous."

I didn't want him to struggle because of me. It wouldn't be right.

He slid his hand onto my wrist, the one I was resting my head on. He rubbed his thumb along my chin, his touch so intimate it made the downy hairs on the back of my neck stand on end, then took both of my hands into his. He made me feel warm. Wanted.

"Sometimes you come to a turning point in life," he said. "Things seem bad but they have a way of working out. Don't rush it. Take some time, a few days, whatever you need. Let things settle."

"You seem so chilled."

"Nope, I am *so* not chilled. I never stop working, for one thing."

I raised my eyebrows. "So this advice is coming from a workaholic?"

He smiled. "You say that like it's a bad thing."

"Then from where? Is that the voice of experience?"

"Something like that."

His eyes lost a little of their glimmer. I'd delved too deep.

"I'm sorry," I said.

"You need to get through today first. What about your sister, Lily? Have you talked to her?"

"It's her day off." My heart lifted. "I could help her look after Thomas."

"Good, because you shouldn't be on your own."

"My car's back at the parking garage, but..." I explained the situation, and Joel offered to walk me to my car.

"That's settled," he said.

"We should probably get going."

I stood because I'd already taken up enough of his time. I could phone Lily while we walked. It was heartening to know someone would drop everything for me. Like Joel had.

As he slid out of the booth, I stepped in his direction too quickly, bumping into him.

"I'm sorry," I said.

He didn't move away, his hands sliding slowly toward me as he cupped my face in his hands and held my gaze. It took my breath away. So close. Anything could happen. He pressed his mouth against mine, his lips warm and reassuring, everything I wanted right now. I kissed him back.

"Don't ever be sorry, Scarlett."

He took my hand into his and led me out of Mario's onto the street. Suddenly I wished he didn't have a job to go back to either so we could spend more time together.

That was when it hit me. Lily had been the first person I'd gone to when I'd broken up with Ronan and found out what he'd done. She was always the first person I called.

Not anymore. Something had changed, something big, and I'd barely even noticed the shift.

CHAPTER SEVEN

Joel

I'd taken the day off work for this. And it was suddenly turning to shit. I could feel it, smell it, sense it.

I'd learned the bass lines for a dozen Merchants' songs before getting here, just like they'd asked, and at first it seemed everything was going fine. I'd made a few mistakes, sure, but that was only to be expected.

The main thing was that my bass had locked in to Cooper's drumming right from the start. He'd even said so himself. Drums and bass as one tight unit, that was what you wanted.

But the mood had changed and I had no clue what the fuck was going on. Cooper had been throwing himself into the drumming, much more keen than the other two, full of energy. Until suddenly he wasn't.

His long hair hung over his face as he sat behind the drums, the sticks in his hand. We were between songs so he didn't need to be doing anything. Still, there was something in the slump of his shoulders and the sudden exhaustion that had taken over him that seemed strange.

"How are you doing over there, Cooper?" I asked.

He nodded, shook the hair from his face. "Fine."

"I think maybe we should call it a day," Lachie interjected.

My gut clenched. *No, no*, please don't let this be the end of it. I couldn't leave them on a low note. That'd be all they'd remember.

"One more song." Cooper turned to me. "Do you know *A Question of Mine?*"

I nodded. "Yup, it was on the list Nick gave me."

No way would I have turned up unprepared. I'd been going through the songs every evening after work with the bass plugged into the computer, playing along with the headphones on. I'd made sure to leave work on time every day, which was enough to make my colleagues wonder what was going on.

And I'd dragged myself away from Scarlett after dinner every evening, forced myself to go to the spare room with my bass and my list of songs, because I'd somehow found myself stuck between two things I wanted.

I wanted Scarlett. I wanted The Merchants. I wanted it all.

Shit, I should have my mind on the music. I was blowing it.

At the end, I said, "Sorry, guys, can we try that one more time?"

I should relax but the more I told myself that, the more tense I became. *Relax, you idiot.*

"Sure thing," Cooper said, and I could have kissed him. He seemed to be my only ally here.

I had to turn this around. Lachie opened with a cool guitar riff, then Cooper and I came in. I had it. Finally, I had it. Nick joined in later, his words floating on top of the song. *Don't think, Joel. Just play.* So I did.

"How was that?" I asked after we were done.

"Heaps better," Cooper said. Maybe he really did want me to kiss him.

Still, that didn't mean I was good enough, that I'd gotten the gig, nowhere near it if the looks on Lachie and Nick's faces were anything to go by. My heart dropped a rung.

"Uh, that was good thanks." Lachie looked down as he unplugged the lead from his guitar, unable to look me in the eye.

Silence. The uncomfortable kind. What the hell could I say to get these guys on my side?

Nick put his microphone down on the table, next to his two guitars, an electric and an acoustic. Masterson's rooms were a step up from most rehearsal places because they were clean and carpeted with walls lined with acoustic eggshell sound foam. I'd been here before, not that the familiarity seemed to be helping.

Nick leaned against the table. "Look, we should probably let you know we've got a couple of other bass players coming around too."

I swallowed. "Sure."

Just because Domino was out of the picture didn't mean there weren't other bass players in Frankston. Or in the rest of the country. Or the world. Because there were guys from all over who'd kill for this gig. Desperation clawed away inside me but I couldn't let it show.

"Don't get me wrong," Nick added. "We like what we've seen."

Not enough, though. Not nearly enough. I had to give it one final effort. I couldn't let this big chance slip through my fingers.

I gathered every ounce of remaining energy. "Can I borrow your acoustic?"

Nick shrugged. "Sure. What for?"

"I'll play you a song I've been working on."

He passed me his guitar and I started playing and singing along. I was taking a risk. This was what I called a 'heartstrings number', a song in the vein of *Everlong,* one that touched people, not a huge rock number and not a typical Merchants' number.

During my late night song-learning sessions, I'd been inspired. I'd thought of Scarlett, and the music and words had followed in a way they never had with other girlfriends. Except Scarlett wasn't a girlfriend.

Breathless, I stopped. The song didn't have a finish yet so I had to break off at some random spot.

Cooper came out from behind the drum kit. "That was really something."

Nick nodded. "I like it."

Lachie leaned against his amp. "Yeah, yeah, it's good. But do we need a third songwriter? You know, too many cooks and all that."

Maybe I was stepping on his toes. I could keep my songs, do something else with them, if they wanted me in the band. *If.*

I handed Nick his guitar. It wasn't a problem if a band had too many good songs. What a load of bullshit. I gritted my teeth as I checked my phone. Scarlett was on her way, nearly here, she said. Something to look forward to.

What did it matter about The Merchants anyway? I'd given it my best shot, and what was done was done. The timing was particularly crap with Black Paisley breaking up.

Maybe that was the problem.

No, it wasn't and no point trying to kid myself. It ate away at me. No matter what else happened in my life, this would always be the one that got away. And I couldn't bear it.

A knock at the door, then Scarlett appeared in the doorway. A boat-necked striped T-shirt showed off the line of her shoulders, a pair of skinny jeans hugging those shapely hips. How could one woman look so amazing with so much flesh covered?

And such a relief to have her here for support. I often talked to my dad about band stuff, but he was away. The whole family was, and it left a hole.

Nick went to the door, gave Scarlett a kiss on the cheek that she returned.

"Nice to see you guys," she said.

Lachie practically leaped across to kiss her and then she wandered over to greet Cooper. I might not be a part of The Merchants but I wasn't missing out on this, so I stepped closer, the two of us exchanging quick kisses on the cheek. A shy smile crept to Scarlett's lips, my reward.

She pointed to the table in the corner of the room. "Ooh, is that a new guitar, Nick? Did you finally get that special guitar you were after? The one with the signature thing."

His face fell. "No such luck."

"It's a bit of a sore point with Nick," Cooper said to me. "He's been hoping for a signature guitar for years."

"Can you blame me?" Nick spread his arms. "Everyone else seems to have their own signature guitar. There's the Taylor Swift model, the Brian Setzer model, the St Vincent signature guitar. Hey, she's a great player but I'm pretty good too."

"You'll live." Cooper and Lachie both grinned. Must be an in-joke with them.

"Um, anyway, this is exciting." Scarlett looked around the room. "My first rehearsal."

"I dunno how exciting it is," Lachie said. "I didn't know you were coming."

"I invited her," Nick said. "Sister-in-law privileges."

Which was only partly true. I'd suggested it, encouraged her, wanted her near.

"Hey." She pointed a finger at Nick. "I'm not officially your sister-in-law yet, not until you're married."

"Good enough as," he said. "I'll be glad when all this wedding stuff is over. The plans and organization are killing me."

Scarlett raised her eyebrows. "But Lily's the one doing all the work. She's organized the caterers, officiant, photographer, the lot. With help from me and Mom, of course."

"It just seems like so much trouble. Maybe it would've been easier to elope."

Scarlett shot him a dirty look. "Really?"

"Hey, I want to marry Lily. It's this whole wedding thing that's doing my head in. As far as I'm concerned Lily and I are married already. We're committed. I sure as hell am. We just don't have the piece of paper yet."

Yep, that was where the problem lay. Why did you have to be committed? Why couldn't you just continue in a relationship without that particular hassle? I didn't say anything, didn't think my thoughts would be welcome.

"Okay," Scarlett said. "You're off the hook. For now."

Nick rolled his eyes. "Women!"

"So, how did everything go today?"

I swallowed. An innocent question, but she could have no idea of the answer.

"Great." Nick couldn't have been more non-committal if he tried. "We might just hang around here for a bit, chew the fat a little longer."

I knew exactly what he meant, and he wasn't including me, so I edged past Scarlett to reach for my gear.

She kept looking at Nick. "So you're not going straight home?"

"Nope."

"You're packing up?" She glanced down at the case for my bass.

"Yep," I said.

"Then I'll meet you outside." A smile and a wave for the others. "Nice seeing you all again."

Scarlett left. She was on my side, I was sure of it, but that wasn't much help when it came to getting a gig with The Merchants.

Time to cut my losses. I wheeled my pushcart closer and lifted the amplifier onto it. The thing weighed a ton. With the bass case in my other hand, I could make it out in one fell swoop.

Nick stepped closer. "How are you getting along with her?"

"With Scarlett?" Why would he be asking?

He gave me a knowing look. "I hope you're cleaning up after yourself, keeping the place tidy. She's a bit of a neat freak."

"A bit..." He had no idea of the previous state of my house. I'd almost forgotten that Scarlett used to live at his place. But it was time to go. "Thanks for everything. Let me know how it goes."

"Yeah, we'll be in touch," Nick said.

Lachie and Cooper said goodbye, and I left them to it, wheeling the pushcart out the door and taking my disappointment with me.

Outside, Scarlett was leaning against the wall in the shade. She leaped across as soon as she saw me, her short blond hair shining in the sun, teeth gleaming. Once again, she was a beacon of all that was good in the world.

"Would you like to go for a coffee?" I asked because that had been our plan, or mine, anyway.

Her shoulders dropped. "I thought I'd drop by and see Lily and Thomas while they were on their own. Before Nick gets back. For some girl time."

"No problem. I've got to dump my gear at home anyway."

"We can go for a coffee later." She gave me that shy smile. "Or a drink."

I put down my bass, let the pushcart rest, determined that at least one thing was going to go my way today. Stepping closer, I cradled the back of Scarlett's head in my hands and pressed a kiss to her lips. I pulled away slowly, taking pleasure in the glow of her skin, the warmth of her brown eyes as she looked at up at me through lowered lashes.

This was the second time I'd kissed her like this. The third time I'd do it properly.

"I'll be ready for that drink whenever you are."

And I left.

CHAPTER EIGHT

Scarlett

It was Friday, normally the end of the work week. Not for me, though. I'd been unemployed for a total of five days and had never been busier.

I had no clue that job hunting and writing applications was a full-time occupation. I'd updated my résumé, phoned several contacts, and had a few coffee catch-ups, all while still working on my portfolio. I'd been thinking about Joel all day too, hadn't been able to help it.

Kneeling in front of the coffee table in the living room, papers in piles, drawings spread out on the floor, the familiar sound of the click of a key in the lock floated through the air, followed by the swish of the door, and Joel calling out. He had his own life, I got that. Still my heart swelled at his return.

He stood in the doorway, satchel slung across his chest. "Whoa, don't tell me you've been making a mess."

"Only a temporary one. Just while I sort a few things out."

"Don't look so shocked. Or guilty."

I threw my hands up. "I can't help it. Besides, I'll tidy

up soon."

"I'm sure you will." Joel dropped down onto one of the club chairs. "How was your day?"

I smiled. The way he said it made me feel like he cared. "I should be asking you that. You're the one who's been at work all day."

"I'm glad to leave it all behind. The others went out for drinks."

"Not you?"

"I decided I'd rather come home. It's good to leave early."

For me? Was there any chance he'd left early for me? I shouldn't think it.

"Wow, leaving early *and* you had a day off this week." I smiled. "What's the world coming to?"

His gaze shifted to the papers and drawings. "So how's the job hunting going?"

"No actual jobs in sight, but it's going okay, I guess. I feel like I've been spending all my time putting out fires."

I'd been through this with Joel before. No matter what Margaret had done—or what her husband *wasn't* doing because he'd washed his hands of everything—I didn't think it right to leave the clients hanging so I'd called all the current customers to let them know the business had closed.

Luckily our biggest project of the year had been finalized last week, so that was one thing crossed off my list. Unfortunately, several other projects were partway through and that made for a tricky situation when things went wrong. And something always did—the wrong tiles would be delivered or the bentwood chairs would suddenly be out of stock.

Joel held my gaze. "You look stressed."

I nodded. The guy was a mind reader.

He stood, slinging off his satchel and depositing it on the chair as he meandered over to the sofa. Settling behind me, he placed his hands on my shoulders. "You're all tense."

More so now that he was close to me, my heart rate rising, only this was the sort of tense I didn't mind.

He started making little circles in my shoulders with his thumbs.

"Oh." The sound escaped my lips.

I closed my eyes as he massaged my shoulders, squeezing out the knots, kept on rubbing until I started to relax.

I let out a long sigh. "That's so good."

"Excellent, because that's the whole idea."

He leaned closer. The warmth of his breath on my neck sent a sizzle up my spine and opened up my senses, my neck arching involuntarily.

Was this what roommates did for each other? A neck and shoulder massage at the end of the day? Because Joel absolutely did not feel like a roommate.

When he was done, I slid up onto the sofa to join him, officially in a state somewhere between relaxed and jittery. I wanted to get closer to Joel and I didn't. Didn't know what was going inside me.

My phone rang, so I reached for it under a pile of papers on the coffee table. A client. At this time of the evening on a Friday. And this person wasn't even officially a client anymore because Intricate Interiors has ceased business.

Joel must've seen the look on my face because he said,

"You don't have to answer it. I'm sure it's nothing that can't wait till Monday."

"You're right." I stared at the phone, struggling for a few moments before putting it down on the coffee table.

He held my gaze. "We could go out to dinner somewhere, what do you think?"

"That's a lovely idea." My shoulders slumped at the thought because somehow I didn't want to share him with a roomful of people. "But I don't feel quite ready to face the world at the moment."

"What about me? Can you face me?"

I nodded, heat pooling deep in my belly that had nothing to do with dinner.

"Okay then, I can cook," he said.

My eyes widened. "You can?"

So far, Joel had ordered takeout for us on the nights I hadn't cooked. I enjoyed cooking so it was no hassle for me. Also, he'd always done his share, cleaned up the kitchen afterward, and tidied the house while he was waiting.

"Of course I can cook," he said. "No way would my mom let me leave the family home without passing on a few family recipes."

"So it's Indian? I love curry."

"Do you like it hot?"

I nodded. I absolutely did. In every way.

He raised his eyebrows. "Think you can handle a vindaloo?"

"No problem."

"You're in for a treat, then."

I felt so at home here and at the same time, it was exciting to find out new things about Joel. Not that I should have been surprised about the Indian cooking. His mom was Indian, after all.

Meanwhile we'd spent all this time talking about me and I didn't know anything that had happened to him, other than the fact that he hadn't gone out for drinks. It had been a couple of days since he'd auditioned with The Merchants. He hadn't said much about it but I sensed how much was riding on this.

"Have you heard from Nick?" I asked.

Joel shook his head, his face hardening.

"I could talk to him," I offered.

"It's better if you don't."

"Okay."

I felt for him, truly I did, and wished I could help.

He stood. "I'll get started on dinner. You need some time for yourself. Why don't you do some yoga? You said you always feel calm afterward."

"That's a great idea." I got up too, frowning at the mess in the room, mess I'd made.

"Leave it," Joel said. "Yoga first."

Bending over, I consolidated two piles of paper. "Okay, I'll just—"

He placed his hand my arm. "You'll stop right there. Yoga, remember?"

I straightened. "Y-yep, got it."

As soon as he let go of my arm, I felt the loss of his touch. I wanted him to touch me. It made me feel petite, warm, and wanted.

Glancing back from the doorway, I saw Joel's eyes were on me, his gaze appreciative, my senses smoking all over again.

Yoga, I had to think about yoga, so left. I got changed,

unrolled the mat in my bedroom, and found my favorite yoga instructor, Tara Stiles, on YouTube. Soon I was in another world, following the moves, not thinking about anything else. By the end of the routine, I felt relaxed, on the inside and out.

As soon as I came out of the shower, I got a whiff of something spicy so I followed my nose, walking through the living room with a sudden newfound ability to ignore the mess around me. Chili, cumin, coriander, I couldn't quite make out the mix of smells, only that they were sensational.

A hand on my chest, I leaned in the doorway, doing some deep breathing. "That smells fantastic."

"And tastes even better." Joel leaned over the stove, spoon in hand as blew on the contents, then slid the spoon into his mouth before tossing it in the sink. "Perfect timing."

"Anything I can do to help?"

"You can take a seat."

I slid down onto a chair, noticed the table had already been set. Joel finished off in the kitchen and brought over traditional Indian copper bowls filled with rice, dahl, and the vindaloo he'd mentioned earlier.

"Cute bowls," I said. "Like you get in a restaurant."

He placed some rice on our plates, then passed me the vindaloo. "You said you liked it hot."

"Absolutely." Flavor burst onto my taste buds with the first mouthful. "That's amazing. So much depth to the flavor. And the lamb is so tender."

"I can get you some milk or yogurt if it's too spicy."

I shook my head and kept eating, despite the cumulative effect of the chili. "Honestly, this is as good as any curry I've had in a restaurant."

"Have some dahl instead if that's too hot."

"I might take a rest." No way was I giving up, not when the vindaloo in particular tasted so good. "So this is your mom's recipe?"

"Kind of. She got it from her father. Gramps used to run an Indian restaurant."

"Really? Here in Frankston? Which one?"

His face clouded over. "The Curry Leaf, but you wouldn't have heard of it. The place closed down ages ago. After Gramps passed away."

"I'm sorry, I didn't realize."

"That was seventeen years ago."

The sadness glimmering in his eyes told me how much he still loved him. So touching to see his sensitive side.

"Can I ask what happened?"

He leaned back in his chair. "A car accident. Gramps was still in his sixties and way too young to go, but at least he didn't suffer. He died instantly."

I covered his hand with mine. "No, it's the people who are left who suffer."

"You got that right."

"My dad died young too." He'd only been forty-five but I didn't want to turn this into a competition. "It makes me realize how precious life is."

"Another thing you got right."

And also how precarious, the part I didn't add. Somehow my dad's death had left me with a vulnerability, a problem when it came to trusting others, and then when I did, I got it wrong. Like with Ronan.

"Are you okay?" Joel asked.

"Yeah, sure." I sipped my water. "Did I mention I

used to live with a guy?"

He shook his head.

"It didn't end well. We'd been together for a couple of years when I found out Ronan was cheating on me. So that was the end of that."

"I'm sorry. What a horrible thing to do to someone." Joel reached for my hand, gave it a squeeze. "The guy was an idiot and an asshole."

I straightened, tried to be strong. "You won't get any argument from me."

"I lived with a girl once too. Mia. For about a year. That was a record for me."

I wasn't sure what to make of that. Somehow a year didn't seem like a long time in the scheme of things, not for someone Joel's age.

"Then I bought this place," he said. "And it was just me and Dave after that. Not very romantic."

Was it romantic, just the two of us? Was he feeling this too?

I alternated mouthfuls of vindaloo, which thankfully had cooled down, with mouthfuls of water while we talked and ate. When we were done, I started clearing the table and picked up one of the plates.

His hand brushed against mine as he reached for it, the warmth of his touch making me stop. I shouldn't feel this, shouldn't be feeling anything.

Joel looked into my eyes. "I'll do it."

"Together," I said.

I couldn't believe that even cleaning up after dinner with Joel was fun. Together. That was the whole point. It hadn't felt this way with Ronan. We'd split the chores down the middle but if I was tired or busy or plain old premenstrual, he would never step over the halfway line and do a little extra. Looking back, it'd been closer to a business arrangement, something I hadn't been able to see at the time because I'd been so stupidly in love with him.

Joel slung a dish towel over the rail. "Did I mention I make a mean martini?"

My eyes lit up. "Then be mean to me. Be as mean as you like."

He sidled closer. "I could never be mean to you."

I let out a long slow sigh. I could fall for a guy like him. Could end up crazy head over heels. Could so easily end up in bed with him, naked, my hands on that magnificent chest, his hands all over me.

"How do you like it?" he asked.

"Sorry?"

"How do you like your martini?"

"Oh, surprise me."

I usually went for sweet girly drinks or creamy cocktails and wasn't sure I'd even tried a martini.

"Stirred, please," I added because that was the only thing I knew about martinis, that James Bond had got it wrong about the whole shaken not stirred thing.

"Of course."

I watched as he poured gin and vermouth into a shaker with ice, and stirred, then carefully tipped the mixture into two cocktail glasses. He didn't have olives so he decorated the glasses with lemon twists instead.

"Perfect," I said as he handed me one.

"You don't know that yet."

"It looks pretty good."

Like him. A man who cleaned up after himself, who cooked, who made martinis, who looked pretty damn good even while he was simply standing there. My breath caught in my throat.

"Why don't we take these outside?" he suggested.

Fresh air sounded like a good idea. Outside, we talked. And talked. Later we had another martini. They were growing on me.

He mentioned that he'd stayed in Frankston, hopeful about getting an audition with The Merchants, while the rest of his family was on vacation in India.

"You haven't told me much about them," I said.

"I'm close to the people who matter, my folks and my brother. Mom and Dad moved out here from New Jersey years ago, mostly because she found the rest of the family too stifling. My grandparents followed close behind. I'm glad my folks moved to Frankston. I wouldn't be 'me' if I hadn't grown up here."

"Do you think?"

"For sure. We're stuck in the middle of nowhere so we do our own thing here, create our own fun. We can't catch a train in to New York City to see the latest bands so we have to start our own bands."

"I guess so."

"Also, after the car accident, I had to spend a lot of time at home. That was when I started drawing and painting because I was on my own so much. So, for me, isolation and creativity go together."

"Sorry, what car accident?"

His expression became pained. "I was in the car with Gramps."

I let that sink in. He was there when his grandfather died. How devastating. And he'd only been a little kid. My heart broke for him.

"But I don't want to talk about that now." He added with a forced smile. "We can always talk about how amazing my vindaloo was."

"Yep, and with enough leftovers for both of us."

As we kept chatting, it turned out we knew some of the same people. Joel made graphic design and interior architecture sound so similar, not that they produced the same results, but in terms of the creative process.

The hours passed and tiredness tugged away inside me, made me feel restless, all this talk reminding me I didn't have a job anymore.

"What's up?" Joel asked.

Maybe he could read my mind or maybe my silence was a clue something was wrong.

I threw my hands up. "It's just that I don't know who I am if I'm not an interior architect."

"That's easy." He leaned closer. "You're Scarlett Novak, beautiful, intelligent, talented, and between jobs at the moment. There's nothing wrong with that."

"It feels wrong, though. Feels like crap."

"I know."

Reaching across, he stroked my hair, made me feel clever and creative and all the things he said I was. Beautiful too, he'd thrown that in. Heat pooled deep in my belly. I wanted him.

And I didn't trust myself. I wasn't a good judge of character. I mean, look at Ronan, at Margaret, both of them had let me down. My heart stuttered at the memory of what Ronan had done and how devastated I'd been.

I needed more time. That was it. Time to think. If things didn't work out, I'd be in a worse position than before. This was Joel's house, after all, and he wouldn't be the one moving out.

As he leaned across, I saw it coming. That was the worst thing of all, I saw it coming and did nothing. Joel slid his hand along my jaw, cupping my face, while I stared into those soft brown eyes and the lashes that were being lowered as he brought his mouth upon mine.

My lips parted. An impulse. And I kissed him right back. A deep desire. I let the kiss go on and on, didn't want it to end.

Eventually he pulled away, took my hand, and I stood. The hunger glimmering in his eyes told me what was coming. And I wanted it too, that was the whole problem.

I could stop at one kiss. I should stop.

"Good night, Joel."

I wandered away from the kitchen. He followed me through the living room where I stopped. What a mess. My mess, my papers and drawings that I'd left scattered across the room.

He sidled up behind me. "You can leave this here."

I bit my tongue. He didn't know me. I couldn't live this way.

"I'll just—"

He reached for my arm. "Leave it. No one's going to die because of a few papers on the coffee table."

"O-okay." I pulled away, my skin still tingling at his touch. "I can always tidy up in the morning."

"Or not at all."

I can be a different person. No, I couldn't. I could only be me.

Edging away, I left before it was too late.

CHAPTER NINE

Joel

We lived together, saw each other every day, so close and yet so far, but this wasn't 'every day'. This was the beginning and I couldn't bear to let a beautiful chance like this go.

"Scarlett."

She'd turned on the bathroom light, lingering in the doorway, the angle of her body emphasizing her breasts. Those boobs. That body. She was so much more than the sum of her parts. She was … everything.

I sidled close to her and switched off the light, my hand sliding across the soft skin of her upper arm. Her lips parted, her gaze lowered.

Leaning close, I nuzzled against her cheek, pressed a gentle kiss to her temple, then another. I peppered little kisses all the way down to her neck, enjoying the way she lifted her head, the warmth of her skin. Bare skin, I wanted more of it.

Cupping the back of her head in one hand, I touched my lips against hers. Gently. Making her wait. I pulled back, saw desire glimmering in her eyes. It took all my self-control not to rip her clothes off right there and then, and take her in the doorway.

Slow, take it slow.

I trailed my fingers along her pretty little shoulder and down her arm. Taking her hand into mine, I lifted it to my mouth and kissed the back of it, then her palm and down along her wrist.

She snaked both hands behind the back of my neck and pulled my head down, brought my mouth crashing down upon hers. Hot and hungry, the kiss was everything I wanted. No more doubts. No more wasting time.

I took her hand, led her to the bedroom. Light filtered in through the wide-open drapes. Her room was in pristine condition, the bed made, of course, the bed we were going to mess up.

Her lips were on my mouth again, her hands on my waist, under my shirt, ripping apart the buttons, pulling it off. She took a moment, the look on her face telling me she liked what she saw. As much as I enjoyed her eyes on me, it was her hands I wanted all over my body. And mine all over hers.

She reached for the hem of her T-shirt, pulled it over her head, unhooked her bra, let it fall to the floor. My eyes were bursting out of my head, my hands reaching forward to take those magnificent boobs into my hands. Soft. Lush. Everything a woman should be.

We ripped off the rest of our clothes, bodies pressed against each other, two people who were made for each other. We fell onto the bed like that, rolling around, skin on skin, a tangle of limbs.

My need for her grew with every passing moment till it was positively painful. She wrapped her hand around my cock and I felt ready to explode but, no, I was going to do this for her. Scarlett first, then me.

I pushed her over onto her back, rolled on top of her, and took those hardened nipples into my mouth, first one, then the other. My hands traveled over her boobs, her waist, her hips, her thighs, her everywhere. I trailed little kisses down her ribs, rising. Along her flat stomach. Lower, lower still.

As I went down on her, I took pleasure in every little moan as she writhed beneath my mouth, in every gasp, in her body tensing as she pressed herself up against me, in the catch in her breath and her final cry.

I dug a condom out of the pocket of my jeans lying on the floor, made my way back up beside Scarlett, wrapped my arms around her, and gave her a few moments to recover. She let out a little whimper.

A few moments felt like an eternity because I was still ready to explode. She took care of that, took care of me, slid her leg over, and took me inside her. The way she was moving on top of me, oh man, this was too much. Those boobs were too much. I took them into my hands, kneading them.

Then everything was too much. Scarlett let out a little cry of pleasure that tipped me over the edge and I came, my body shattering into a thousand pieces, a thousand wonderful pieces.

We lay together for a while. We went at it again. We talked. I could talk to her all night. I could go at it all night. I could stay like this forever. I'd always liked this room and it seemed there was plenty of space for both of us.

I didn't even know how this had happened. She'd become a part of my life, moved in, given me so much without even trying.

"You're an incredible woman, Scarlett," I whispered.

Images flashed in my mind, Scarlett surrounded by papers in the living room, on the back porch martini in hand, sprawled across the bed, naked in front of me. Most of all, naked. And breakfast in the morning, that would happen too.

We drifted off to sleep.

*   *   *

Light came streaming into the room early in the morning, waking us both way too early for a Saturday morning. Still, that only meant we had more time together.

Birds twittered in the oak tree as we ate breakfast on the back porch, toast and coffee, because not every meal had to be fancy. Scarlett had thrown on a pair of shorts and a tank top. No bra. I could get used to this.

Something had happened and it had nothing to do with the lack of a bra or the boobs, though both of those things were amazing. Deep inside me, something had shifted. It wasn't the sex. I'd had girlfriends, had sex before, had been in relationships, even though I'd been good at avoiding getting in too deep.

But now there was no turning back.

It was Scarlett. I didn't want her to leave. Ever. Such a scary thought.

I knocked back the last of the coffee in my mug, placing it on the table between us. "You're very quiet this morning. I hope everything was all right last night."

"Last night was *very* all right." She threw her head back and laughed. "It couldn't have been more all right. It's just, I've had a lot on my mind, a lot of big changes in my life, moving into this house, losing my job, looking for more work."

I'd had a lot on my mind too, work, music, the band, Scarlett. I wanted to help her, damn it, in any way I could.

"You could always set up on your own," I said. "Start your own business."

"Me?"

"Yes, you. Remember what I said last night about you being intelligent and talented."

She smiled. "Beautiful too, you forgot that."

"Goes without saying. I mean it. You're good at your job. You're dedicated. You've shown your loyalty to your old clients even when you weren't obligated. You're smart, Scarlett, too smart to be left lingering too long."

"It's only been a week."

"I didn't mean it that way. I only meant that if you wanted to set up as a freelancer, you've got all the skills. It just depends on what you want to do."

A cute furrow formed in her otherwise perfect brow, her 'thinking' face. It didn't last long though, her expression becoming increasingly content. Her shoulders relaxed too, so different from yesterday afternoon when I'd come home and she'd been a stressed-out mess.

"I'd need clients," she said. "Margaret was the one who pulled in all the business."

"Your old clients would be a good starting point. For one thing, you can charge them for any work you do for them from now on to finish off those existing projects. I'm sure they know your services are worth paying for."

"Nice of you to say."

I held her gaze. "I'm not being nice, Scarlett. I'm being truthful and I'm certain you can do this."

She got that cute little furrow again. "I'll need

somewhere to work. It's not often that clients came to the studio, but I'll still need room for my computer and my things, space to spread out."

I nodded in the direction of the shed. "I've got just the thing."

She looked at me, then at the shed, her mind ticking over.

Getting to her feet, she took my hand, breathless now. "Let's take a look."

My sense of anticipation heightened as we ambled toward the shed, still holding hands. Because that was what this was about. The two of us.

The grass looked a bit the worse for wear by the double front doors. I could always add some paving to make a small landing for a more welcoming entry. Or maybe I was getting ahead of myself.

I pulled open the door because I hadn't bothered to keep it locked, not since Dave had left and taken all his stuff with him. Right now, I couldn't have been more thankful that I'd let him use this space for storage because it meant it was empty now.

Scarlett wandered inside, looking the place up and down. There wasn't much to see, just a large empty room with entry through a set of double doors and a window that looked out onto the yard.

"It needs a good cleaning," I said.

She glanced up. "I'll have to paint the ceiling first, work my way from the top down." She slid her fingers along one wall, then wiped them on her shorts. "I know exactly the sort of wood paneling that'd be perfect for a feature wall. It looks like old pallets. Imagine the contrast if the other walls are crisp white with the light streaming in. It'll add exactly the right ambiance."

See, that was the thing. When Dave had been living here, we'd never had any ambiance. There'd been no 'we'. Now I was a part of something. And soon we were going to have ambiance. Excitement coursed through me.

"We'd need to take care of all the preparations first." I didn't want Scarlett high up a ladder sanding the ceiling. I could take care of that.

She bit her lip, a shy look overcoming her face. "Are you sure?"

"About what?"

"That it's okay if I take over the shed and use it as my studio."

She'd already taken over my mind and my body. What difference would it make if she took over a shed that I wasn't using?

And maybe it meant she'd hang around for a while, maybe even for a long time. The thought shocked me. I didn't know what I was thinking or doing anymore. I'd never wanted any woman as a permanent fixture in my life. It wasn't me, wasn't the way I worked.

I'd rather be on the big stage, playing in The Merchants, living the dream, only that dream that seemed so far away. I sighed.

"I think it's perfect timing," I said. "You're setting up your own business. You need a space to work. And here it is."

She kissed me and squeezed my hand, jiggling up and down with excitement. The sight of those boobs bouncing was too much for me. I tried to contain myself.

"I'll need to buy paint, get a few other things from Home Depot…" Her voice drifted off.

"We can do that."

"We?" Her lips curved to that shy smile I liked so much. "You'll help?"

"Of course."

She placed her hands on her hips. "I'll need to stop by the studio—sorry, my *old* studio—to pick up a few things, samples mostly and I'll need to download some files, paperwork from councils, some other stuff."

"I'll come with you." I didn't want her going on her own. Just in case.

"And I need to grab a few things from Lily's. Is that okay?"

"Sure."

She reached for my hand. "I'll text her. She'll be up early anyway. Probably Nick too, whether he likes it or not."

Nick. I should speak to him, try to find out where I stood. My heart dropped because I wanted an answer about The Merchants and I didn't.

Scarlett texted her sister and got ready in record time, which was a huge disappointment because she put on a bra to leave the house.

We took my Volvo because the V70 was bigger than her Mazda. Scarlett prattled away in the car, excited at the prospect of starting her own business, jumping from one idea to the next, comfortable with thinking out loud in front of me.

"It's funny," she said as we pulled up to Nick and Lily's place.

"What?"

It took until we were walking up the front path for her to answer. "When we first met, I thought you'd have a cool car, maybe something vintage. You know, since you're a graphic designer. Your studio is a funky warehouse and your house has all those mid-century pieces. Meanwhile your car is a Volvo. So safe."

"Do you have any idea how heavy a bass amp is?"

"Nope."

"Or how big?"

She tilted her head. "Actually, I noticed how big."

"The car might be boring but it does the trick."

Excited now. "Ooh, in that case, maybe we could come back later for my desk and some shelves."

"We'll see."

I couldn't make this woman out. One minute she was insulting my car and the next she was filling it up with more gear. Didn't matter, though. I liked the way her mind worked. I liked everything about her.

Lily opened the door and let us in. In some ways the two sisters looked similar—same eyes and cheekbones, the same expressions—then there was the difference in height and hair color.

Sprawled across the living room sofa, Nick's bleary eyes told me he wasn't a morning person. He introduced me to Thomas, seated in front of a coffee table covered in drawings and pencils while a pile of LEGOs lay on the rug beside him.

Nick got up, looked at Scarlett. "Do you need a hand?"

Thomas tugged at his leg. "Daddy, Daddy, you were going to help me with my drawing."

I crouched down by the coffee table, thinking I could get this over with quickly. "Maybe I can help. Are you any good at coloring?"

He nodded. "Very good."

"If I draw Superman, do you think you could color him in?"

He nodded earnestly, handing me a blank sheet of paper while I picked up a marker and drew the world's quickest outline of Superman. I'd had enough practice as a kid.

Yep, six months recuperating at home after the car crash had given me plenty of time to draw superheroes and cartoon characters before moving on to develop my own style. I'd had some company from my brother but he'd had to go to school of course, and I'd needed more. A lonely time. And I'd never become used to it.

Thomas's eyes widened. "Wow. Thank you."

"That's awesome," Lily said.

"Thanks, Joel," Nick said. "Scarlett's old room is this way."

Lily stayed with Thomas while Nick charged ahead of me and Scarlett.

"I didn't know you liked kids," she said.

"Who said I liked kids?"

"You were great with Thomas."

We stood in the doorway while Nick went into the bedroom. She had this all wrong. Kids were fine in small doses, then I was done.

"Drawing and LEGOs, I can handle," I said. "But the whole responsibility thing when it comes to kids is way too much for me."

Scarlett raised her eyebrows. "Really?"

Nick handed Scarlett a box. "This one isn't too heavy."

"Got it." She gave me a strange look as she turned and left.

I had other things to worry about. The Merchants. Dread dragged me down, fear of being turned down, but I had to ask, especially since we were practically face-to-face.

I turned to Nick. "Have you guys come to a decision?"

He looked blank, then frowned, took his time. "About a bass player?"

I nodded.

He held a hand out. "Oh, sorry, man. I've got a lot on my plate with renovations at the bar, and Lily is nonstop with the wedding plans. It's one thing after another."

I bit back my resentment. As much as I hated being strung along, going off at him about it wasn't going to help.

"I'll give you a call early next week," Nick said. "Maybe we can meet at The Swamp."

"Sure." I lifted a box. "Next week."

Next week, next month, next year. Didn't make a lot of difference. I was still left hanging, but at least I had Scarlett.

CHAPTER TEN

Scarlett

Champagne on a Wednesday night, what could be better? I could sleep in tomorrow if I wanted. More likely I'd get up early because Joel had to go to work.

I was trying to ease the cork off the bottle, struggling if I was going to be honest, because you could never tell when the darn thing would fly off and that always made me squirm.

"Would you like me to take care of it?" Joel asked.

I passed him the Veuve while we sat side by side on my leather sofa, small enough that it had fit into Joel's Volvo. It sat at one end of my new studio, leaving plenty of room for my desk, the centerpiece of the room, taking pride position and providing a lovely view through the window. During the day, that was.

Joel pointed the bottle toward the corner of the room. "Get ready!"

I squealed as the cork shot across the room, bounced on the wall and rebounded off the desk till it eventually found a place in the corner.

"Good shot," I said.

"Aren't you going to pick it up? We can't have any mess lying around. Wouldn't be professional."

"Nope, I'm going to leave it." I straightened. "I'm starting a collection."

"Of champagne corks?"

"Why not?"

He poured the champagne and handed me a glass. "To Scarlett Interiors."

Joel had come up with the name. I'd liked it instantly, loved the play on my name and the color scarlet and had even referred to myself as a scarlet woman. Joel was also going to help get a website up and running, but it was one thing at a time.

I sipped my champagne. "Aren't you going to ask me what we're celebrating?"

He leaned back. "I did ask. Lots of times."

Which was true. I'd only found out late this afternoon myself and hadn't wanted to tell him when he'd come home from work tired because he'd been sorting out some problems. It had taken all my self-control to make it this far.

I placed my glass on the coffee table, cleared my throat. "I had a phone call this afternoon and…"

"And?"

Forget about self-control. I did a seated running man, jiggling my feet on the floor. "I got my first proper client today!"

Joel put his glass on the table and threw his arms around me. "That's fantastic."

He held me tight. I loved his hugs, the way he teased me. Loved everything about him.

Eventually, he pulled away. "I'm so happy for you.

Your first client, the first of many."

I nodded, couldn't stop grinning. "Have you heard of a guy called Adrian Barr?"

"The one who owns Stables Restaurant?"

"Yep, well, he wants to move away from fine dining into cafes and a more casual market. And he needs an interior architect. When he phoned, he said he'd had trouble tracking Margaret down, so I explained what had happened. And he said that was fine by him because he wanted *me* to do the interiors. He'd seen my work, and wanted me on board. He didn't even need to think about it."

"The guy has been in business a while. He probably trusts his gut."

I squirmed, unable to keep still. "It's so exciting. This'll be the first café and then he says there'll be many more. So there'll be heaps more work coming my way. The emphasis is on funky interiors to attract a hipster crowd. This is *so* up my alley. And he wants each café to be individual but still with a linking theme."

"Have you discussed your fees?"

The one thing I wasn't comfortable with. "I have to do up a quote."

"Do you know what Margaret would charge for a project like that?"

"Yeah, she wasn't cheap."

"Then you've got to charge the same amount."

"But I don't have her experience, her longevity."

"You were the one who did all the designing. She wouldn't have had a business without you. Don't underestimate your clients or undersell yourself."

I wasn't sure what was reasonable but I'd certainly give

it some thought.

Joel picked up his glass, handed me mine. "A toast." He pressed a kiss to my lips. "To Scarlett, beautiful, intelligent, talented, and now I can add also 'successful businesswoman' to the list. I'll need more adjectives soon."

I gave him a shy smile. "I don't know how much of a success I am yet, but this is a beginning. I haven't called Lily. I wanted to tell you first. Wanted to make it a bit of an announcement."

He sipped his champagne. "We should do this every night."

"I wish I had good news every night."

"You will. Things will work out for you."

"What about you?" I chewed on my lip. "Has Nick got back to you?"

Joel shook his head. "I don't have an answer yet. He asked me to meet him at The Swamp on Friday. Would you come along too? For moral support."

I clapped a hand to my mouth. "Oh, there's something important I forgot to tell you. You're invited to the wedding as my guest. I'm in the bridal party but I'd be thrilled if you could be there. And so would Nick and Lily."

He squeezed my hand. "Sure, I'd love to. I was secretly hoping…"

"Hoping what?"

"Being invited to the wedding is fantastic but it doesn't mean I'm in the band."

I nodded. Because he was right.

"I get the way it works," he said. "They need to make sure they get the right guy for the band. I only hope that's me. And if they go with someone else…" He dropped his head into one hand. "It's not worth thinking about it."

I didn't want him to feel down. "You've still got your job at Chemistry Design and you're very good at what you do."

His Adam's apple bobbed up and down as he swallowed. "But I'd give it away in a heartbeat for a band like The Merchants. Don't get me wrong. I like my job. But I *love* my music. It's what I live for. And I've put so much energy into it for so many years."

I shrugged. "Sorry, I was trying to look at the positives."

"And I appreciate it. You're right. I've got so many good things in my life. You, for one."

I wasn't his Number One, though, far from it. My heart sank. Because maybe I wanted to be his One and Only. Because I was falling for him faster than I had for anyone else. And deep in my gut, I knew there would be Before Joel and After Joel. Only I couldn't bear to think about the 'after'.

Placing his glass on the table, he cupped my face in his hands and lowered his mouth over mine, made me feel wanted, made me believe everything would be all right. I deepened the kiss, tongues rolling, the yearning inside me growing.

I wanted to believe. Damn it, I wanted to believe.

He held me in his arms. "This is your celebration. You deserve it."

"Things have turned around for me pretty quickly."

"Because you're clever and you're trying to make the best of a bad situation. You're not scared of hard work either. Look at what you've done in here in such a short time."

"You helped." Joel hadn't been scared of a bit of hard work either.

"And you did an excellent job with the wood paneling."

A highlight of the room, if I did say so myself.

"I'm a mean hand with a miter saw and a cordless drill." These were some of the things I'd picked up from Lily's place on the weekend. As soon as we'd started talking about transforming the shed into a studio, I'd known I'd need my tools.

"You're incredibly handy around the house."

"I had to be. Dad died when I was thirteen so after that, it was only me and Mom and Lily at home. Someone had to fix things around the home, and I was the oldest."

"What about your mom?"

"She did everything else."

"So where'd you learn this stuff?"

"One of my uncles showed me. He used to help out a lot and I hung around him. Even when I was a kid, I thought I should know how to change a light bulb and drill a hole in the wall. It grew from there. Then Uncle Joe would buy me power tools as birthday presents."

"And you liked that?"

"Are you kidding? I loved it."

Joel squeezed my shoulder. "See, that's what I like about you. You're not like other women."

"You've helped me a lot."

"Nah, you were never going to be homeless. We've been through that."

"You've helped me find a new side to myself."

Joel was the one who'd suggested I start on my own in the first place. He'd believed in me when I'd thought it would be safer simply to keep looking for another job. I didn't have a nine-to-five now. I had something better.

And I wasn't working from a desk in my bedroom or a cupboard in the hallway. I had an awesome studio. These were all things I'd dreamed for myself for one day in the future. I just hadn't thought they'd happen so soon.

"I'm not just Scarlett anymore," I said. "I'm Scarlett Interiors and I couldn't have done it without you."

"All you needed was a little nudge."

I looked around the room. "This was a bit more than that."

"I think you're loosening up a little too."

"Loosening up? Excuse me?"

"I didn't mean it in a bad way. You're not so uptight if there's a bit of a mess around."

"Okay, I can be a bit of a neat freak, but that's not such a bad thing. At least I'm not a slob."

"See, I'm not taking it personally if you think I was a slob when you first got here. It's a question of balance."

"I'm *extremely* balanced. Watch this." I leaned forward, purposely pushing over a neat pile of interior magazines. "See."

"That's a good start."

"And the champagne cork in the corner. That's messy. And I'm leaving it there."

His eyes narrowed. "That's ... not exactly a huge mess."

"I'll give you a mess."

I stood, ambled over to the other side of the coffee table, ripped off my T-shirt, and tossed it to the floor. "I'm going to leave that there too."

It wouldn't make any difference to Joel but I hated

seeing dirty clothes strewn across the floor. It went against everything I believed in.

He leaned back, stretching his arms across the back of the sofa. "What else are you going to do, since you're such a terrible slob?"

"I... I'm... " I looked around, picked up the Veuve. "I'm going to drink straight from the bottle."

Joel grinned. "Go on."

I stared at the bottle in my hand, thought about how this would leave germs on the rim. No backing out. I knocked back a big slug of champagne, then another. It tasted pretty good this way, and what were a few germs between friends anyway?

He laughed. "Excellent."

"I can do even better."

My hand shaking, I brought the bottle to my lips again, thought about letting it dribble down my chin but couldn't bring myself to do it. I stopped. Joel was looking at me so expectantly. I had to do something, so I tilted my head back and tipped champagne over my chest.

Still smiling, he didn't budge from the sofa. "Such a waste of perfectly good champagne."

I tipped a little more over myself so my bra was soaked. And transparent. At least I hoped it was.

"Why don't you come closer and lick it off?"

His eyes burning with desire, Joel stood, moving slowly toward me to kiss me on the mouth. My neck arched as he trailed little kisses down my neck, then hooked a finger under the strap of my bra and let it fall over my shoulder, first one, then the other.

His mouth was on my collarbone, lower onto my chest, lower still while he was licking and sucking, his mouth on my breasts, his hands too. He took one nipple into his mouth, his other hand kneading my breast. Desire coursed through my body. I was ready to let him take me there and then. Nearly.

I shoved the champagne bottle into his hand. I'd show him who was messy, who didn't care, who left their clothes lying around the entire house.

"Wait," I said. "Not too fast."

My gaze glued to his, I took a few steps back, then wandered into the yard, my hips swinging. Turning back to face him, I saw his shocked expression as he stood in the light, bottle still in hand.

I slid my hands behind me, unhooked my bra, held it up for him to see, then tossed it to the ground. Looking over my shoulder as I headed into the house, I motioned for him to join me.

I lost my shorts in the living room, threw them onto the coffee table. Slid my panties off in the hall. Like Hansel and Gretel, leaving a trail. I draped myself across the bed. I'd never felt so exposed, nerve endings on edge, my whole body tingling.

Tingling turned to thrumming as Joel walked into the room, his mouth open, breathing heavily. He shucked off his clothes, didn't say a word. Said it all with his body. With the way he kissed me, deep and long. With the way he touched me, gently at first, then with more urgency. With the way he moved on top of me, taking his weight onto his arms. With the way he slipped inside me, our two bodies moving as one.

He held me afterward, as he always did. Held me close, then gave me space when I needed it.

It had happened so quickly, this thing between us, this

relationship that had exploded out of nowhere. Joel had been spending every night in my room, only going back to his room for clothes, and I liked it that way.

I rested my head on his chest. "This feels so right."

"Damned straight, it does."

"You're not going to go back to your room, are you?"

"No, why would I?"

"Just checking."

He pressed a kiss to my hair. "Scarlett, you know how special you are."

Did I? Sure, I was special but that didn't mean I knew how I fit into the scheme of things or what he wanted out of the relationship, maybe not right now but further down the road.

Meanwhile, I knew. No doubts. This was love. That was why I felt this clutching at my heart, this high I was riding, the longing that took over me, this need to be with Joel all the time.

My self-preservation instincts kicked in. I couldn't say it, not until I knew he felt the same way.

"There was something about you from the first moment I saw you," he said.

Something? Would that 'something' be enough for me when I yearned for him to love me back?

I forced a smile to my face. "I think it might've taken a bit longer than that."

"No way, I thought you were a babe."

"No, you didn't. The first time you saw me was at Lachie's party. That wasn't exactly our finest moment. You thought I was a pain."

"The most beautiful pain I've ever come across."

"Gee, thanks." I rolled onto my back. "It feels like that

was so long ago."

"It was."

"And we've come such a long way."

"Yeah." The most non-committal 'yeah' I'd ever heard.

"My world has certainly changed." In more ways than one. "I'm working for myself, running a business, and I've got my first big project on board. I can see where this is headed. What about you? Where do you want to be in a few years time?"

"On stage with The Merchants."

He didn't even need to think about it.

"What about us? Where do you see us headed?"

He sat up in bed, frowning. "In a few years time?"

I stayed where I was, pulled the sheet up. "It was just a question."

We hadn't been seeing each other very long, but he was twenty-seven. Surely he'd at least thought about whether he'd like to be in a relationship and how he'd like his life to pan out.

"Let's keep things the way they are," he said.

"Sure." I swallowed. "I'm happy with the way things are for now."

"Good, because lots of things can happen."

True. He could be accepted into The Merchants and that would be wonderful. It didn't mean I couldn't be a part of his life as well. It certainly didn't mean he couldn't think about more than one thing at once.

Damn it, if he had hopes, then so did I.

I rolled over and pressed my eyes shut. I'd done enough talking for one night.

CHAPTER ELEVEN

Joel

The sun blazing outside, it was a relief to walk into The Swamp with Scarlett at my side. Nick stood by the bar talking to Austin, their old bass player. Was there some reason for his presence, like maybe he was coming back to the band? My nerves stood on edge.

"Joel, this is Austin," Nick said.

I shook his hand, told myself he was into rockabilly, and that was why he'd left the band. With his bowling shirt and his quiff, he didn't even look like the other guys.

Scarlett waved and said hello to the two of them rather than greeting them with a kiss. I couldn't have been more glad she was here.

"We were just discussing the new bar," Nick said. "Sorry, I thought we would've been finished by now."

Such a relief. Austin was his architect for the project. I knew that, only I'd forgotten. Still, it didn't mean *I* was going to be their new bass player.

I still couldn't believe Austin had left The Merchants to resume his career in architecture. A band like The Merchants was the dream. Then, maybe his dream was something else.

"I still think banquette seating would look good against that wall," Nick said.

"Yes, but banquettes take up a lot of room." Austin may have been saying yes, but his face was saying no.

"They're really cool," Nick said. "Everyone wants to sit in a booth."

Austin's expression stayed serious. "We can do it. I'm not saying we can't. I'm just saying they take up a lot of floor space."

"Maybe I can help." The sound of Scarlett's voice made them look her way. "Layouts and interiors are my specialty."

Austin smiled, or maybe grimaced.

"I'm just saying there are ways of incorporating banquettes that are more economical in terms of floor space," she said. "And it might be worth it for the extra income in food and drink consumption per square foot."

"I'm aware of that," Austin said.

She shrugged. "I don't want to step on your toes. It was just a thought."

Nick piped up. "I gotta say I like the sound of that."

A smile crept to Scarlett's lips. A small win, perhaps.

Austin looked at her. "You know the whole place is going to change when the renovations are underway?"

She nodded. "I've seen the plans. Nick's been through it with me."

"Has he now?"

"And I love what you're doing. Moving and remodeling the bar is going to be a huge improvement, and it was a smart move to renovate the bathrooms before doing anything else, especially given the planning delays with council and all that stuff. You know exactly what you're doing, no doubt about it."

"Thank you."

"How are things going with the loose furniture, the stools and tables?"

He held a hand out. "Fine."

I was tempted to jump in and tell him just how good Scarlett's work was and how much she'd been doing for Margaret's old clients—who were now her clients, of course—except Scarlett got in first.

"I can help with that," she said. "It's what I do every day, whereas you might not be aware of the options and suppliers."

"What's up, Scarlett?" Nick said. "I didn't know you were interested in The Swamp."

"I've started up my own business," she said. "Things are different now."

"Well, it's all under control." Austin's phone rang. He said a few words into the phone, then stepped back, motioning for Nick to join him. "It's the carpenter."

I nudged Scarlett. "I didn't know you were going to bring that up now."

"Bring what up?"

"Trying to get a job out of this."

She shrugged her pretty shoulder. "It only just occurred to me. I know that sounds weird but Margaret was always the one who brought in the clients so now I have to get into a completely different mindset."

"Maybe you could talk to Nick about it another time. I mean, you see him when you visit your sister."

"Austin's not there though, is he? And he's the architect."

"It's just … I was hoping to use this time to find out if they'll have me in the band."

Her expression hardened. "And that's more important than what I want?"

"I didn't say that. Nick asked me here to talk about the band, or at least I thought he did."

"Maybe we don't want the same things."

The simplicity of her words, the finality of her tone, the complacency in her face hit me like a ton of bricks. My stomach twisted into a knot. *Not now. Don't do this now.* Yet somehow I sensed this was something that had been playing on her mind for a while.

"Come on, Scarlett, that'd be a silly thing to start an argument about now."

"I'm not arguing. It was just an observation."

Somehow I doubted it.

Nick came back. "Glad we've got that sorted."

"I've got to go," Austin said. "Nice meeting you, Joel. I'll see you again, Scarlett."

"Yes," she said. "At the wedding."

Austin left and Scarlett wandered toward the band room.

"Where are you going?" I asked.

"Nowhere," she said over her shoulder.

Nerves rumbled in my stomach at the thought of being alone with Nick. This was nuts. Time with him was exactly what I'd wanted when I'd walked through that door. An answer, more to the point, but I was worried it wouldn't be the answer I wanted.

I nodded toward the band room, waving for him to join me. This might be a conversation that was easier to have while walking. It also might be over very quickly.

"I didn't come here to talk about the bar." I pulled my shoulders back, forced myself to stand up straight. "I'm more interested in The Merchants."

He raked a hand through his hair. "Oh, yeah, sure. Sorry about that. I've had a lot on my mind with the bar and the wedding, especially the wedding."

"Thanks for the invitation. I really appreciate it."

"No problem. Lily insisted and, hey, who am I to argue?"

"Great." I hoped I didn't sound too sarcastic, hoped Nick was pleased to have me there too, even if it was only as Scarlett's guest.

"Lachie and I are still trying to get some more songs together. We want to be able to pick the cream of the crop for the new album. You know what I mean?"

I nodded. That'd be my dream. To be a part of The Merchants, to play on the album and—while I was dreaming—to have one or two of my songs on the new CD.

So close and yet so far.

Nick picked up where he'd left off. "And The Flats is coming up after that. A gig like that is big even for us. I mean, this is our town and everything."

I nodded. "I get it."

The Salt Flats Festival wasn't as huge as Lollapalooza or Coachella, but it was ours and that meant something. I'd played The Flats with Black Paisley—as one of the first bands on during the day so the crowd was small—and even so, it'd felt so different from other gigs. Anyway that wasn't the band I was thinking of.

"And The Merchants are headlining," I added.

"Sure are." He shoved his hands into his pockets.

"Look, there are lots of reasons why I don't have an answer for you yet, but I can't go into it all."

My heart sank. I couldn't fucking believe it. How long were these guys going to keep putting me off? My chest rising with anger and frustration, I clenched my fists to stop myself from losing it.

Nick must've seen the look on my face because he stepped closer, spoke in a low voice. "Some other stuff has come up too. We don't really want to talk about it but Cooper is having a few problems, and it's making things tricky for all of us."

"What sort of stuff?"

Lips thin, he struggled with his words. "Look, I can't talk about it and I'd rather Scarlett didn't know either."

At that moment, Scarlett turned to look at us. If she'd been pissed off before, she'd gotten over it. "Decided to join me, have you?"

Nick stopped beside her. "Yeah, I guess we have."

"You're not changing the band room too much then, are you?" She wandered inside.

We followed. I'd seen a lot of bands here. I'd played here often enough too, long before I'd started Black Paisley. Even when it was empty, the room was filled with music. You could feel it. The room was dripping with it.

"I've always liked the black walls," I said.

Scarlett nodded. "Me too."

I raised my eyebrows. "It doesn't affect your delicate design sensibilities?"

She laughed, took it the right way.

"I don't want to change too much in here," Nick said. "Best to keep it simple."

"I always thought a mural would work on that wall

over there. Something dark and murky." This place brought back memories, lots of them. "I did a mural at another bar a few years ago. Sorry, not a mural. A painting."

Nick's mouth fell open. "You're not talking about the one at The Silver Swallow, are you?"

"Yeah."

His eyes widened. "That big black and white artwork in the huge brass frame?"

"Yeah, that's the one. That was a few years ago. I haven't done any painting in a while."

"You're kidding. I love that painting."

"Really? That's great."

He pointed toward the wall. "So what did you have in mind?"

I had to think on the spot. "It's just a vague idea, not something I've thought about much. It'd have to be a huge, mother-sized thing, something that was in-your-face and sat in the background at the same time. Something that encapsulated the history, the bands that have played here, the vibe, and creativity of the city."

Nick nodded. He was actually thinking about it, giving this serious consideration when it was just some random idea that had floated out of my mouth. It also wasn't the matter I wanted him to be considering.

Scarlett broke the silence. "Joel is an amazing artist. He can do anything he sets his mind to."

"Thanks." Guilt flooded through me. Scarlett had the grace to compliment my work while I hadn't done a thing to stick up for her earlier. A big mistake.

"So will you do it?" Nick asked.

It was tempting. Might help me get inside with Nick,

which could work in my favor. Or it could have absolutely no impact on whatever decision the band came to.

"This is a bit quick," I said. "Don't you need to check with your architect or something?"

"Honestly, Nick." Scarlett cut in. "I think a mural would be the perfect, stand-out piece."

Hell, I had a job and a band and a girlfriend. Didn't even know if I'd have time for an artwork spanning a huge wall. None of this was working out the way I'd hoped it would.

Still, maybe I could make something of it. "I'll think about it, Nick, but I really need to discuss the project with your *interior* architect."

He turned to Scarlett. "Look, I can't guarantee Austin needs your help. I don't even know how this stuff works."

She planted her hands on her hips. "Austin's a great architect, I'm not saying he's not, but I'm good at interiors. It's what I do. His expertise isn't in the soft furnishings or different types of barstools, not to mention the commissioned pieces."

A muscle in Nick's jaw flinched. "Scarlett..."

She waited. A stand-off. Scarlett had known Nick a long time and I had a feeling the two of them had been here before. You needed more than a knife to cut the tension. A machete, perhaps.

"You're busting my ass again, Scarlett," Nick said.

Her lips tightened. "Not at all. I'm telling it like it is."

He threw his hands up. "I'll see what I can do, but I can't make any guarantees. Austin's my architect and you've come into this late in the game."

"Not too late."

"I've gotta go." He shook my hand. Leaning over, he

kissed Scarlett on the cheek, a braver man than me.

As he was leaving, I turned to her. "I've got to get back to work too."

"Sure you do."

"What's that supposed to mean?"

"You three were ganging up on me back there."

I shook my head. "No, we weren't."

"Maybe not." She folded her arms. "I'm the one who needs clients, who needs this interiors project, but you're the one who's getting the mural. How is that fair?"

I spread my arms. "I had no clue that was going to happen. It was just an idea, not even a serious suggestion. Besides, that wasn't why I came here."

Her eyes blazed. "No, but it's what happened. How could you?"

She turned and left before I'd even registered what was going on.

Now I knew how Nick felt. A guy getting his ass busted.

CHAPTER TWELVE

Scarlett

After that day at The Swamp, Joel had done all the right things after doing all the wrong things. He'd called me from work and we'd talked through a few issues, not that we'd come to any sort of agreement, except on the fact we didn't want to be mad at each other.

We'd had a wonderful weekend together too, a lazy weekend for a change, one that involved lounging around and drinks with friends and a movie night at home. And sex. There'd been plenty of that.

Now the weekend was well and truly over. After getting stuck at work, Joel had texted to say he was on his way back with pizza. My favorite pizza from Massimiliano's to be more specific, with mozzarella, Swiss cheese, chicken, and roasted peppers.

I'd already poured red wine into glasses. Hearing the familiar sound of his key in the door, I grabbed knives and forks from the drawer and placed the cutlery by the plates.

"I'm in here," I yelled.

"So am I."

Joel appeared in the doorway, pizza box in hand, his

hair mussed up, looking as scrumptious as I'd ever seen him. My heart melted just a little.

He placed the box on the table, gave me a quick kiss on the lips. A bit more heart-melting happened.

"Sorry I'm late." He sat down, lifted the lid. "Is it okay if we get started?"

"Definitely."

He slid a piece onto my plate, then served himself. "And wine too. That's a nice touch." After his first bite of pizza, he said, "Tell me about your day. What've you been up to this afternoon?"

I sipped my wine. "I didn't have much actual work to do. Though that'll change, I'm sure. So I just tidied the place up instead."

His eyes wandered around the room. "I thought it looked different in here."

It should. I'd gotten rid of the clutter from the bench tops, canisters, and such, before getting started on the cupboards and making my way through to the living room. I'd had the time and plenty of nervous energy to use up.

I could pretend to be messy but that's all it was— pretending. The real 'me' was a neat freak and always would be.

Both of us hungry, we polished off the meal in record time.

"The pizza was awesome." I pushed away my empty plate.

Joel got up. "I might get a drink of water. Do you want one?"

"No thanks."

He opened the cupboard door, reached inside, then stopped. "Where are the glasses?"

"I moved them."

He raised his eyebrows. "You moved them?"

"They're on the high shelf to the right of the sink."

He stood and grabbed a glass from the cupboard. "And why are they there?"

"Because it's more convenient. You get a glass and you're right there by the sink next to the tap. Like you, now."

He was already pouring himself a glass as he turned, then took a sip. "Okay, I guess so."

"I rearranged all the kitchen things."

"Really?"

"So everything's in a more logical place now. The pots are next to the stove, glasses near the sink, plates under the main countertop."

He put his glass down and opened the cupboards, looking inside four or five of them before giving up. This was my place now too. Or that was what I'd been thinking when I was in the midst of a cleaning frenzy this afternoon.

I shrank back into my seat. "Is that okay?"

"Sure." He leaned against the countertop, tilted his head. "Is this ... some sort of punishment?"

"What? No. I thought I was helping."

He nodded. "That's great, thanks."

"You'll get used to it. Besides, being neat and tidy isn't a punishment. That's such a strange thing for you to say."

"It's fine, really."

He closed the lid of the empty pizza box.

I edged forward, ready to get up. "I'll take that outside."

"Can we just leave it? No one's going to die if the

pizza box is hanging around overnight."

"S-sure."

I didn't want to push it. I may already have gone too far by rearranging the kitchen, but I'd thought he'd appreciate a woman's touch.

He ran his fingers through his long hair. "All this can stay as it is for now. I'll clean everything up in the morning. We're both tired so let's go relax in the living room with a coffee."

"Okay."

"I'll make the coffee. You've already done so much today."

A loaded compliment if I'd ever heard one. I gritted my teeth, letting it pass. Maybe he was right and I should learn to relax more, so I took a deep breath, wandered into the living room, and settled on the sofa.

A few minutes later, Joel came in with two mugs of coffee. "Here you go."

I edged closer as he sat down. I liked being next to him and the last thing I wanted was another stupid argument.

He frowned, looked around the room, then pointed to the cabinet that sat along one wall. "What happened to the rosewood box?"

"That old thing?"

The cabinet, a classic mid-century piece, was minimal like the other furnishings in the room whereas the trinket box was a fussy timber thing with elephants carved in the lid, and simply didn't go.

"What?" He jumped up, his hands on the edge of the cabinet as if his presence could miraculously bring the box back.

"I put it away."

He leaned over the cabinet, his shoulders slumped with relief. "Thank Christ for that."

"It's inside on the top shelf to the right."

Joel retrieved the item, cupping it in both hands as he slid it onto the center of the cabinet. "You have no idea how much this means to me."

My gut tightened. As far as I knew, tidying up wasn't a crime but I'd obviously crossed a line.

I swallowed. "I'm sorry. I made a mistake. This is your place, after all."

"It's your place too." He ambled back over to the sofa and sat beside me. "That box might look like some cheap, tacky, Indian thing but Gramps gave it to me when I was a kid. It's the only thing I have from him, other than the memories."

"It's not tacky." No, *I* was the one who was tacky. "I'm sorry, Joel. I had no idea."

"I panicked. I thought you might've thrown it out."

"No, I'd never do that." Especially since he'd said he stored some old jewelry in there, not that I'd opened the box to look. It wasn't any of my business.

I remembered the pain in his voice when he'd talked about his grandfather. "You were close to Gramps, weren't you?"

He nodded. "I was always hanging out with him. When I could, I'd go with him to buy produce for the restaurant. That's what we were doing when ... when the crash happened."

A pang cut through my heart. "I can't imagine what that must've been like for you."

"It was partly my fault." He looked down. "The crash,

that is. I was singing some stupid song, making a hell of a noise and being a general nuisance. We were at a 'yield' sign but Gramps was distracted. Because of me. The car got T-boned at an intersection. Also because of me."

I took his hand into mine. "It wasn't your fault, Joel. You were just a kid."

"I know that now, but at the time, I felt like I was being punished for it. In the car, I didn't get it right away, didn't understand Gramps had died. I understood later, though. Then I got some crazy infection during my hospital stay. It kept me out of school for months, at home alone with my mom. Like a jail sentence."

"That's a long time for a kid."

"It was a hell of a long time to be without friends."

"But you must've had friends."

He grimaced. "A couple of them visited me. At first. Then it became too much trouble for them so they didn't bother. I can't tell you how lonely I was."

I felt for him, for a poor kid abandoned by his friends. "That must've been tough."

"So when I went back to school, I had to make friends all over again. If I'm a nice guy, it's because I had to be. I worked hard at it."

"You're a great guy. If that makes you feel any better."

"It's okay. I'm over it."

I didn't believe that for a minute. More likely, this was something that had shaped him. I squeezed his hand.

"Well, the trinket box should definitely stay on top of the cabinet," I said, trying to brighten my voice. "It makes for an interesting juxtaposition of styles."

He cracked a smile. "An interesting ... *what*?"

"It looks great up there."

"You hate it."

"No, I'm looking at it in a different light now."

"I think we can meet halfway on some things."

I nodded. "If you're talking about me being a neat freak, I'm trying my hardest. I don't panic when there's one thing out of place anymore. I've come a long way, truly I have."

"So have I."

I let his words sink in. Maybe I hadn't given Joel enough credit. A stab of regret cut through me.

"You're right, and maybe I should be more appreciative. It's not a matter of life or death. We can find a middle ground, something that's not fastidious and not slob-like."

"Hey, who said I was a slob?" He grinned. "Maybe you can tell me about the rest of your day."

There *was* no 'rest of my day', so I said, "No, why don't you fill me in on yours?"

He told me about the latest drama at work where a client had hit the roof about something, so it'd been all hands on deck in revising the designs. Hence his late return home.

I settled back into the sofa with my coffee. "I'm taking Lily to the final fitting for her dress tomorrow."

"I thought she'd already had one of those."

"No, the dress was still a bit loose around the waist so they had to take it in a smidge and that affected the boning which meant it was a bigger job than it should've been."

"Did the dress really look that bad? It's just a dress. I mean, it's not a matter of life or death. Like you were saying before."

I edged away. "It's her wedding dress and everyone

will be looking at her. What's more, the wedding is this weekend."

"And I'm sure she'll look beautiful, but it's still just a dress she'll wear for one day."

"So we're back to 'just a dress'?"

"That's exactly what it is. A huge fuss for one day and then it's over."

I had an inkling, more than an inkling, that he thought weddings were more trouble than they were worth, that people needn't bother with them, that they were a waste of time. And money too perhaps.

"Is that really what you think?" I asked.

"Look, it's great that Nick and Lily are getting married if that's what they want. It's their business, not anything to do with me. But Nick's been pissing me off when it comes to an answer about me joining the band."

"Maybe Nick should've given you an answer by now. That's not fair. And just so you know, I think if the answer was an outright no, they'd have told you by now. 'No' is quick. I don't know why the rest is taking so long."

"Yeah, well, I'm trying not to get my hopes up."

The look on his face told me he was failing. I had a pretty good idea how much he wanted to join The Merchants, and it was somewhere close to the life-and-death-category.

I cleared my throat. "My point is, you can't blame the wedding for that. You can't wish Nick and Lily weren't getting married because of it."

"I'm not."

"It's a tad selfish, Joel."

"Yeah, maybe it is. I'll admit it. There are times it's okay to be selfish."

I could see what he meant and where he was coming from. Still, something about his tone bothered me, something that went deeper.

"Besides," I said, "they're not really making a huge fuss about their wedding. They're keeping things as simple as they can."

"True. No bachelor party,, bachelorette party, or bridal shower. I'd have thought Nick might want some of that stuff, being a big musician and all."

"Maybe it's *because* he's a rock star that he doesn't want a huge fuss."

Only one groomsman. Lachie, was going to be best man. And I was the only bridesmaid. My sister's maid-of-honor, and it was truly my honor. My heart swelled because this meant so much to me.

"Lily wants to keep things simple too," I said. "She just wants to tie the knot. They've got Thomas and now they've got a commitment."

"Which is great for them."

It was only the last two words I heard. *For them*. And maybe that was what bothered me.

At first I'd thought Joel seemed highly committed—to his job, for one thing, until he said he'd quit at the drop of a hat to join The Merchants. I'd seen no sign of commitment to previous girlfriends. They'd all seemed like flights of fancy. He did seem committed to his family, but that was different somehow, less of a choice.

"Hey," he said. "I can't wait for the wedding. I know how much this means to you and how much you love your sister." He pressed a kiss to my cheek. "She won't be the only one looking beautiful on the day. There's a pretty good chance you'll outshine the bride."

"Nope." I shook my head. "No chance of that."

He nuzzled into my neck, scattering little kisses on my bare skin. I pressed my eyes shut. I ached so badly to be a part of Joel's life, for things to work out, for him to want to have me around not just today and tomorrow, but the day after that. And maybe even the year after. Commitment wasn't such a bad thing.

"I want you to know…" Joel's breath was heavy in my ear, his hand closing over my breast. "That I'll be on my best behavior at the wedding."

"Good," I whispered.

"I'll say nice things about the dress."

He slid his hand under my bra, his fingers warm, searching until he found my nipple. Sensation rippled through my body. I gasped, couldn't help it.

"And I won't try to rip your dress off till much later."

"You talk too much." I could barely get the words out.

He covered my mouth with his, our lips parting, tongues rolling. A sensual shiver shot up my spine, every nerve ending in my body alight. How could he do this? How could it be so quick, so instant, so overwhelming?

Deepening the kiss, he knew exactly how to make me respond. It didn't matter that we hadn't been together very long. He knew every square inch of me. Intimately.

I knew him too. Knew what he liked.

He concentrated on kissing. I concentrated on unbuttoning his shirt and getting it off. Unbuttoning his jeans, I slid my hand inside. Hard, just the way I liked him. He moaned.

Pushing the coffee table aside, I dropped onto my knees on the rug while he got rid of his jeans and sat back down. Naked, also the way I liked him. I found my spot between his legs and took him into my mouth. He wasn't talking too much now. Instead he was groaning, breathing hard. Until he wasn't.

I gave him a few moments, stared at the coffee table askew with the rug bunched up underneath it. I could do messy. I could be just as wild and crazy and messy as the next person.

My gaze glued to his, I edged back onto the rug, hooking my fingers under the hem of my T-shirt. I shucked it off over my head, tossing it across the room. My bra went the same way. I curled my finger, motioning for him to join me.

He didn't need to be asked twice. Joel reached for a condom from his jeans on the floor, then prowled across. Hungry. I needed him too. More than I wanted to admit. Needed him inside me. Needed that particular fire to be put out. Then I'd need him beside me, his arms wrapped around me, his body warm beside mine.

We were so good together, no question about it. I liked the way he was happy to lie beside me after we'd had sex. We'd caress each other gently, chat quietly, or sometimes just lie there.

Small talk, I could do small talk. Then Joel started kissing me again, deep kisses that left me breathless. His hands were on my hips, my waist, my breasts. The way I wanted him so badly brought tears to my eyes, but I wasn't ready to go at it again. Something else was pooling inside me, a sense of melancholy, a touch of sadness bringing me down.

I covered his hand with mine, pulled it away. "Can we just lie here for a bit?"

"Sure." He pressed a kiss to my forehead. "This

wasn't exactly what I had in mind when I bought the rug but it suits me just fine."

He grinned and I smiled right back.

"You'll need this." He reached across the sofa, bringing back a cushion that he tucked behind my head.

"What about you?" I asked.

"I'm fine right here." Lying beside me, he propped himself up on arm, still grinning. "I like the view from here."

His gaze shifted from my face to my breasts, along my body, my legs, and then back again. A sensual shiver shot up my spine. I wanted this. And I wanted more.

Sex wasn't the problem. How could something so amazing be a problem? It also wasn't the answer.

Because I wanted more. I wanted a relationship, something that went beyond today and tomorrow. At the very least, I wanted a foundation of some sort. I wanted to know this would last.

Was it too much to ask for forever? Maybe not now, but one day. Because that was where I was headed, and I wouldn't accept less.

And therein lay the problem.

CHAPTER THIRTEEN

Joel

Nick's parents had decked their yard out in serious style for the wedding, or maybe Lily had organized that. A marquee had been erected over the tennis court with a separate part of the yard set up for the ceremony with about fifty thousand flowers. I'd wandered past on my way to the back door of the house.

Scarlett had just texted me, and we'd talked about it the other day. She wanted me to meet her mom and grandmother before the ceremony, though now I was waiting, I didn't see why it couldn't wait another hour until that was over.

She'd arrived at the house early this morning because, apparently, it took all day to prepare for a wedding. I had no clue what they'd been doing—hair, makeup, nails, how long did that stuff take?

Then I laid eyes on her. Every second had been worth it. She stepped out of the back door, the sight of her in a strapless burgundy gown taking my breath away or, more accurately, it may've been the sight of those boobs in that push-up bra driving all the blood to one part of my body.

I sucked in a deep breath. I'd better get my shit together before I met her mom.

"Come on." Scarlett took my hand, dragging me away.

"I thought I wasn't allowed to see the bride before the wedding."

"You're not."

Stepping inside the house, Scarlett pulled me in with her, looking around to make sure no one else was around. On tiptoes, she cupped my face in her little hands, pulled me closer, and kissed me gently.

"Sorry." She smiled. "Gotta be careful. Don't want to smudge my lipstick."

"Nope, certainly don't want to do that." I held her at arms' length. "You look gorgeous, Scarlett. There's no doubt you and Lily will be the two most beautiful women here."

"So tactful." Her eyes widened. "You cleaned up pretty well yourself. Look at you. Such a lovely shirt. You even shined your shoes."

Because I knew these things mattered to her. Nick had insisted on no suits because it was too damn hot in Nevada, even in the evening, so I was wearing a white shirt with tan pants and a pair of brown leather lace-ups.

"This way." Scarlett nodded for me to follow as she walked into a living room, very formal, where her mom and grandmother were waiting.

The two ladies stood, her mother coming forward for a kiss on the cheek. "Joel, we've heard so much about you."

"I'm so pleased to finally meet you, Sandra."

"And this is Baba," Scarlett said. She'd already primed me that this was what they called her Croatian grandmother and that it would be rude to call her by her first name. No danger of that since I couldn't pronounce it.

The older woman stretched out her arm for a handshake, making sure to keep her distance. "I don't know if I want to kiss you yet."

Luckily, Scarlett had already warned me she could be a bit scary at times.

"Pleased to meet you," I said. "I can see where Scarlett and Lily get their good looks from."

Baba rolled her eyes.

I looked from her to Sandra. "I'm serious. The family resemblance is amazing."

Blushing, Baba reached forward for my arm. "You take me outside. We go now."

"Certainly." I looked at Scarlett. "Where are Nick's mom and dad? Are they around?"

She waved it off. "They're having a quiet gin and tonic before the ceremony."

Which seemed a bit weird since this was their house.

Sandra gave her mother's hand a quick squeeze. "I'll join you shortly, Mama."

This had to be worth serious brownie points. We walked at granny pace which was fine because the woman was, after all, a granny. It gave me plenty of time to look around and take everything in, more than I liked.

When we reached the flowered arch leading to the sectioned-off area for the ceremony, I felt like the father of the bride leading her down the aisle. As if I'd wandered into some strange alternate universe.

At the front, Nick shifted from foot to foot. Lachie nudged him, said something that put him at ease. I'd never seen the two of them dressed so formally, both of them in button shirts with dark pants that looked more like they were more likely to sit in front of a computer at an office than pick up a guitar on stage. They'd cleaned up all right too.

They didn't seem to notice a young woman in a black dress on the other side of them, taking candid shots while they chatted. I'd met Ginger before when she'd photographed a Black Paisley gig.

Finally we made it to the front where I helped Baba to her seat next to an old guy who had to be her husband. The aisle seat was free, for Scarlett's mom no doubt, after she'd walked her other daughter down the aisle.

Baba gave my hand a serious squeeze, didn't want to let go. "This is Dida."

"Nice to meet you," I said.

"You can go now." Baba finally let go of my hand.

I stepped across to shake Nick's hand. "Everything okay? You look nervous."

He wiped the perspiration from his brow. "You have no idea. Getting up on stage at Glastonbury was easier than this. It's the wrong way around. The smaller the crowd, the scarier it is."

Lachie slapped him on the back. "Maybe you should've invited more people."

Nick shook his head. "Only the people who matter."

I took that as a compliment, my chest swelling with appreciation even if I'd only been invited by default. It was still a wedding, still special, for him and Lily.

I wished Nick luck, not that he was going to need it, and made my way toward the back, figuring that if I hid in the back, I'd get a better view of Scarlett as she came down the aisle.

Cooper stepped out as I was passing. "Hey, why don't you join us?"

"Sure."

It might be a relief to be with at least one other familiar person. He took a seat on the other side of an attractive young woman, her arms lean, shoulders sinewy in the strappy dress she was wearing.

"Would you prefer the aisle seat?" I asked her. "You'll get a better view."

She patted the empty seat. "No, I'm fine, thanks."

"This is Jess." Cooper leaned across, then laughed. "We're the leftovers."

I sat down. "Sorry?"

"Jess is Lachie's girlfriend but he's at the front, best man. And I'm just left over."

She punched him lightly. "No, you're not. All it means is you haven't found the right girl yet, Cooper."

Cooper rubbed his arm. "Hey, you hurt me."

"If I hit you, I guarantee you'd know it." She raised her eyebrows. "So in the meantime, you'd better make sure you behave."

It came to me. "Oh, you're..."

Everyone knew about Lachie's stalker and how he'd been attacked outside the radio station. It had made the news across the country. Scarlett had given me the inside story, and explained how Jess was a self-defense expert who'd stopped the woman stalker, fought off some other guy, and diffused the situation. Impressive stuff.

Jess nodded. "Yep, I'm a bodyguard. Well, I *was* Lachie's bodyguard."

"That's cool." I looked at Cooper. "We should be safe

with Jess then."

He laughed.

Ginger stopped partway down the aisle, lifting her camera to point it in our direction.

Cooper held a hand out. "No, no thanks."

I guess he didn't want his photo taken. Meanwhile, Jess motioned for Ginger to come our way. Talk about confusing.

Jess leaned across. "Love the dress. You look like a Korean Audrey Hepburn."

Ginger smiled. "Ooh, I have to get ready." She was off, taking her position closer to the front.

"So, you know Ginger?" I asked.

"Yeah, she's a friend of my roommate's."

It always seemed to work that way in Frankston. Someone always knew someone.

"And she's the official photographer?" I asked.

"Yep."

Cooper said something to Jess that I didn't quite catch.

The first notes rang out from a piano. I looked around, spotted a white baby grand way over to the right at the front. A familiar song.

Nick moved to the center of the aisle, started singing *Maybe I'm Amazed*, the love song Paul McCartney had written for his wife. Talk about a diehard Beatles fan.

The early evening air became still, the hair on the back of my neck standing on end. An eerie moment.

Nick held his arms out, much more comfortable now he was doing the front-man-thing again.

We all stood. Young Thomas came into view, taking careful steps and beaming as he held a velvet cushion bearing the rings secured with ribbons. The kid was so little and there was so much space around him that he made the floral arch look huge. Eyes fixed firmly on his dad, he made his way to the front where Nick ruffled his hair and pulled him closer.

Then Scarlett stepped through the floral arch and walked up the aisle, a small bouquet of white flowers in her hand. A shiver shot up my spine, the sight of her both beautiful and scary. My heart was racing, my face draining of color, and that was saying something for an Indian guy. For a few seconds, I couldn't hear anything, as if the audio had been cut off.

She made her way to the front, her back to me now, and my world went back to normal. Shit, what had happened? We'd talked about how lots of stuff wasn't life or death, but that was what exactly what those moments had felt like. A response to danger. Fight or flight. Not that I was going to fight Scarlett, but fear had cut through me nevertheless.

I shook my head. This was nuts. The next thing I knew Lily was standing at the front and Nick had taken her hands into his, singing the final words of the song.

Scarlett's mom took Thomas's hand, leading him across the aisle to take a seat beside her at the front.

I forced myself to concentrate on the ceremony so I didn't look and feel like such a douche. A gentle breeze washed across the crowd, 'gentle' being the operative word, enough so it helped me breathe. The happy couple exchanged vows, the sky glowing orange and engulfing us all in its warmth as the sun set in the distance.

Those fateful words from the officiant. "You may kiss the bride."

Nick leaned over while Lily stood on tiptoes. The two

of them couldn't have looked happier, glowing more than the sunset as they kissed, followed by a small round of applause. Thomas went running up to them, Nick picked him up, and the crowd clapped more loudly, me included. The happiness levels just went up a notch.

I was happy for them too, but this wasn't for me. It was freaking me out too much.

The two of them—or rather, the three of them—walked back down the aisle and we gathered around to congratulate the newlyweds. The place was like a giant bubble of happiness.

Scarlett found me, gave me a quick kiss on the lips that made all my worries wash away.

"I know." I smiled. "Gotta be careful because of the lipstick."

She was beaming. There was a lot of beaming going on this evening.

"Such a beautiful ceremony," she said.

"Sure was."

A passing waiter handed out glasses of champagne. Now there was an idea. The bubbles slid down my throat. I could get used to this.

Scarlett had already primed me that she'd have to disappear to another part of the garden for the official photos while the rest of the guests were served refreshments. I spotted Austin and said hello. Cooper introduced me to a couple of people. I chatted to him and Jess. I mingled.

Twenty minutes later, Scarlett came up to me and Cooper. She had Austin on one arm, a champagne glass in her other hand.

"That was quick," I said.

"We're not done yet." She turned to Cooper. "I'm on a mission. I need you to come over with us and have your photo taken. Nick wants a picture with all the guys from the band."

He nodded. "Sure."

Austin nudged Scarlett closer to me. "Perhaps you'd like to take over."

"You should come with us." She linked her arm into mine. "You too, Jess. Come on. Tara is over there too."

We wandered across to a secluded part of the garden with an immaculate lawn and a landscaped rockery complete with a small waterfall. Because every house needed one of those.

Jess and Tara stood chatting, while Scarlett and I moved across to get a better view of Ginger organizing the guys into position for a picture of the four of them with the bride.

Ginger sized up the scene, a hand on her hips. "Great, but can we get something that's a bit more rock 'n' roll?"

Nick swept Lily into his arms and the other guys joined in so they were holding her horizontally in their arms. Lily was shocked at first, then laughing, the guys grinning too as Ginger snapped away.

The guys kept hamming it up, Cooper getting down on one knee with a rose between his teeth like a conquistador while Nick kissed Lily and the other two guys struck a pose.

After they were done, Lachie came and joined us. "Hope you didn't mind."

"Mind what?" I shrugged. "Why would I?"

"The band photos were for old times' sake. It's been the four of us for a very long time."

I waved it off. "Nah, that's fine."

"Still, it's not a very warm way to welcome the newest member of the band."

My mouth dropped open. I froze. Surely he couldn't be saying what I thought he was saying. And I couldn't bear it if I'd gotten this wrong. I balled my hands into fists, tried to hold back.

Lachie stared at me. "What? Nick hasn't told you?"

I shook my head. Didn't dare speak.

"He's been all over the place lately," Lachie said. "Frankly, he's had his head up his ass. We should never have trusted him with this." Maybe the silence got to him or maybe it was the look on my face, as he added, "You're in the band."

"I'm…" I spluttered, couldn't get the words out.

Lachie nodded. "You're our new bass player."

A slow grin spread to my face, my whole body filling with warmth, relief, wonder, and a bunch of other emotions I couldn't identify.

Beside me, Scarlett was jumping up and down. Literally. She threw her arms around me and I spun her around. I couldn't believe this was happening. The band of my dreams, the woman of my dreams, everything I'd ever wanted.

"That's fantastic." I put Scarlett down and shook Lachie's hand but couldn't shake the grin from my face.

"Sorry if I was a bit cold that day you jammed with us. Your songs are good. Who knows? The Merchants might be heading into a new era."

Maybe I should have been paying more attention to Lachie but I couldn't help myself. I cupped Scarlett's face in my hands and kissed her.

"Hey," she said. "Lipstick, remember?"

"Oh, sure."

The next moments went by in a blur. I seemed to be doing a lot of blurring today. Lachie wandered off. Scarlett too, as she was called away for more photos.

Cooper came up, whacked me on the shoulder. "Lachie just filled me in. Sorry, I thought you knew. We both did."

I was still grinning. "Well, I know now."

"There are a few other things we need to fill you in on too. Maybe on another day. Now we've got to celebrate." He lifted his glass. "Oh, you don't have one."

"I'll have a glass later. I don't need it right now."

He raised his eyebrows. "And just for the record, I thought the way Lachie talked to you that day you jammed with us was a bit rough."

"Not really," I lied. He'd been extremely weird that day and had pissed me off. Not that I cared anymore. Nothing could bother me right now.

"I think he was a bit jealous," Cooper said.

I stared blankly. "Of what?"

"That song you'd written."

I frowned. "The song I played to you guys? But that's crazy. Why would Lachie be jealous of *my* songwriting?"

Cooper didn't say anything. Just nodded. This was incredibly flattering, even if it couldn't possibly be true. They'd liked my song, that was enough for me. I was The Merchants' new bass player. My life was transformed. Elation buzzed through my veins, my heart pumping fast and strong, every nerve in my body alight in the best way possible.

One thing was for sure. Nothing was going to get me off this high.

CHAPTER FOURTEEN

Scarlett

It was nearing the end of the night, thank goodness, because this had been a long day. Lily's special day. Nick's too, I shouldn't forget that. And I was so glad for both of them, glad I could be there for my sister and absolutely thrilled at how things had worked out for them.

The only thing I hadn't anticipated was how sore my jaw would feel from smiling so much all day. A small price to pay. It'd be funny if not for the small matter of the pain involved.

My eyes wandered around the interior of the wedding marquee. Lily hadn't been sure about it, but the wedding planner and I had convinced her. I'd added a few touches of my own, two trees in giant pots at the entry because the area had the height and could take it. The chandeliers were an inspired touch, helping to fill the roof space. And flowers everywhere because Lily loved flowers and, what the heck, this was a wedding.

Joel and I were relaxing at the bridal table, a round table like the others in the room because Lily had said they wanted to feel like they were a part of the wedding, not the main attraction.

I leaned closer to Joel. "Too many wonderful things have happened today. I couldn't believe it when Nick started singing *Maybe I'm Amazed*. That was so romantic. Such a surprise too. Lily had no idea."

"Yeah, you mentioned that."

"Oh, no, I'm repeating myself, becoming boring."

He pressed a kiss to my cheek. "You could never be boring."

I looked around at the thinning crowd. "A few boring people have left already." I shrugged. "I guess that's fine. It is getting late."

"It's a bit weird that Nick's parents left the party so early. I mean, it's their house. Their son too."

"And this is them on their best behavior."

I'd already explained how Nick's dad hadn't been much of a father and was now trying to make things up to him, which was why they'd offered up the use of their grounds for the wedding. Most houses had a yard. Theirs had 'grounds'.

It was the one thing they'd done for Nick over the years so Lily had said they should make the most of it. And they had.

"I don't think Nick cares that his folks have disappeared." I settled back in my seat, then giggled. "Look at my mom over there, mixing with the guys in the band."

On the other side of the room, Lachie had his arm around Jess, while Nick said something that made my mom crack up. He put his hand on her arm, and somehow that had Mom doubled over with laughter. Lachie and Jess were laughing too, though I wasn't sure if it was at Nick's joke or my mother's reaction.

Determined to enjoy every moment of her daughter's wedding, Mom had arranged for Thomas to have a sleepover at a niece's tonight. I wasn't sure who was more excited, Thomas or my cousin.

And tomorrow Nick and Lily were taking Thomas on their honeymoon with them because he was their child. Because they could. Because they wanted to, and it didn't matter if that wasn't the accepted way of doing things.

Baba and Dida had left not long after dinner, which was fair enough because they were old.

Joel pointed to my mom, still partying with the best of them. "She's lovely."

"Yep, Mom's great and Baba's a hard taskmaster. I can't believe how well you got along with her. That was a huge deal."

"Not really. Must've been my charm and natural charisma."

He couldn't keep the smile from his face so I gave him a playful nudge.

"What about your folks?" I asked.

"What about them?"

"They're back tomorrow, aren't they?"

"Yep, you'll meet them soon. After they've had a couple of days to settle back in, that is. They're going to love you, I'm sure of it."

"Hope so."

Joel put his arm around me. "I know this is their wedding but tonight's really my night. That's how it feels anyway."

"I'm still so happy for you." My lipstick long gone, I pressed my lips against his. "I don't know what was going on with Nick. I still can't believe he didn't get around to telling you that you'd made it into the band. I'll have to have a word with him."

"It doesn't matter so much now."

"It's wonderful news." I tried to think of some more adjectives, amazing, awesome, excellent. "It's like the jewel in the crown for the evening, the icing on the cake, the full kit and caboodle."

Joel squeezed my shoulder. "It's okay, Scarlett. I get the idea."

I pouted, couldn't help myself. "Too many clichés?"

"Maybe, but coming from you, they're cute."

"I'm tired," I said. "It's been a big day."

"Hasn't it?" Joel's dark eyes sparkled. "I can't wait to get together with the guys from the band. Lachie's interested in working on some songs with me."

"Yeah, you mentioned that already." I poked him in the side gently. "Now who's repeating themselves?"

He smiled. "Joining The Merchants is a dream come true."

"And coming out with the clichés too?"

"This is the most important thing in my life. Nothing else compares. It's everything I've ever wanted."

I stiffened, edged away.

"I didn't mean it like that," he said.

"It's okay." My stomach clenched, realization setting in. Because I knew. I'd always known.

"I was talking about bands and music. That's a different sort of thing. You're everything I've ever wanted too. I love being with you."

But I wasn't the most important thing in his life and never would be. I forced myself to look on the bright side, stopped myself from losing it completely. Was it so bad to be second best? The ache in my heart told me the answer.

A spluttered gasp escaped my throat.

Joel placed his hand on my back. "Are you okay?"

I coughed. "Fine. I just need some fresh air, that's all."

He pushed his chair back. "I'll come."

I held a hand out. "No, I'll be fine."

It wasn't far to the door of the marquee. Not far for Joel either, as he followed. I stepped onto the grassed tennis court. The air prickled against my skin. Cool or warm, I couldn't tell which.

Joel came up beside me. "You're upset."

You're a mind reader. The words I didn't say. Lots of words I didn't say.

Damn it, I found it so easy to be blunt with other people and lay the facts down for them. Wasn't so easy when it came to my own life.

I held back the tears burning in my eyes. "Do you have any idea what you said in there?" I threw my hands up. *"Everything you ever wanted. Nothing else compares."*

"It kind of slipped out. I said the wrong thing."

"And you meant it. There are other things you've said, Joel. This isn't the only time." I took a deep breath, steeled myself, held back the crack in my voice. "Where do you see us going, me and you?"

"Why do we need to go anywhere? Things are so good as they are, and they're only getting better with you starting your own business and me joining The Merchants. We're onto something here."

My hands trembling, I balled them into fists, squeezed them tight. I didn't give a shit about the band. Couldn't bear to hear their name again.

"We're living together," I said. "In case you hadn't noticed, you seem to have moved into my room. Doesn't that mean something?"

He placed his hand on my arm. "Sure it does."

I pulled my arm back. "Where do you see yourself in a few years? Where do you see *us*?"

"What's wrong with keeping things the way they are?"

"You can be in a band and still have a meaningful relationship. They're not mutually exclusive. I mean, look at Nick."

A muscle in his jaw flinched. "It's different for him. He's got a kid already."

"What's that supposed to mean?"

"I'm not a commitment kind of guy like Nick. Can't see myself doing … this. It's just not me. I've got so much ahead of me. Things are just falling into place, and I don't want it affecting what we've got."

Damn it, I didn't expect a proposal but I expected something, some small sign. The ache in my chest deepened into pain so severe it took my breath away. It was a struggle to remain standing.

I had to get the hell out of here before I burst into tears. Even if there was no one else outside, this was still way too public a place for this discussion. For any of this.

And I absolutely could not let myself break down during my sister's wedding. No way would I ruin this for Lily.

The next minutes went by in a blur. Kissing and hugging Lily and Nick goodbye, forcing a smile to my face, telling them how late it was and how I should get home. Joel was a pretty good actor too, wishing them well, saying goodbye to people, calling a cab.

We didn't speak in the car. The longest cab ride home ever. The driver didn't say a word either, just grunted, and I couldn't have been more grateful.

I trudged up the front path of the house, no looking back, while Joel paid the driver and raced to catch up with me. His footsteps got louder as I slid the key in the door and pushed it open.

I looked around the darkened hallway. What had I done? I'd let myself get comfortable, fooled myself that this could be my home too, yet somehow I'd wandered into enemy territory.

The warmth of Joel's breath on my neck made the downy hairs on my nape stand on end. I tilted my head up, squeezed my eyes shut. He was going to slide his body against mine and I couldn't let him. Sometimes there was only one way. Head on.

I turned to face him. "I can't do this anymore, Joel."

He held my gaze. Expectant. "Do what?"

"Things are never going to work out between us. This is a mistake."

A frown formed in his brow. "What? We're going to have this discussion standing in the hallway?"

"There's no discussion, Joel. It's over."

He tilted his head, his eyes narrowing, his lips parting in a way that had nothing to do with desire. "You're kidding, aren't you?"

I shook my head.

"I-I thought you were happy, Scarlett."

So had I. Until tonight. The warning signs had been there but I'd been in denial. No more.

"I won't take second best," I said. "I wouldn't take it with Ronan, and I won't accept it now."

"But I'm not seeing someone else. I'd never do that." He grabbed my shoulders, not rough, desperate perhaps. "If it's about what I said tonight, I can make it up to you."

"That's just it. You can't."

I turned and walked away, closing the bedroom door behind me. My room, our room, I didn't know anymore. But it wasn't mine. None of this was mine.

My back pressed against the door, I slid to the floor into a crumpled heap. I let the tears slide down my face, sobs shaking my body as I covered my mouth so I wouldn't make too much noise and all the while hoping for a miracle I knew couldn't happen.

CHAPTER FIFTEEN

Joel

"You can't do this, Scarlett."

I stood in the doorway of her room. Hell, it wasn't that long ago it'd been *our* room, except then it had felt like home and now it looked like a bomb had hit the place. It sure as shit didn't look like anything to do with Scarlett Neat and Tidy Novak.

The closet doors had been flung open, drawers opened, clothes scattered everywhere while Scarlett folded items into piles, laying them into an open suitcase. Empty boxes had been tossed in the corner and around the room, waiting to be filled. I wanted them to stay just the way they were. Empty.

She straightened, looked across at me. "Yes, I can."

Breathless, I struggled to get the words together. "I can still play in The Merchants. We'll tour and we'll come back. Frankston is home to these guys. I'll always come back."

She shifted around a couple of piles of clothing. "I won't be hanging around waiting. I have my own life."

"And I can be a part of it."

She closed the lid of the suitcase, her chest heaving with the exertion. "No, Joel. We don't want the same things."

I stepped inside, then strode back a few feet. The floor covered in stuff, there wasn't even room to pace. Claustrophobic, yes. Messy too. A huge goddamn mess, in fact.

"Is it because I said I wasn't a commitment kind of guy?" I knew the answer, knew how badly I'd screwed up. She didn't say anything. I cleared my throat. "I can change."

She stared or glared, I wasn't sure which.

I was changing right now. Regretting every word that had passed my mouth, every stupid selfish thought.

I raked a hand through my hair. "Maybe I believed it when I said it, but that was only because I'd never found a woman like you before, Scarlett."

The pain clawing at my chest told me that. I'd had plenty of breakups. You'd think I'd be used to it by now, but none had been like this. None had left me sleepless, stomach churning, my heart lurching, and feeling overall like shit.

"Is it just that one small thing?" I asked.

Her lower lip trembled. "It's not small."

My stomach sank even further. "I didn't mean it that way. I meant if it was only one thing, we could work out a way."

She heaved the suitcase to the floor and reached across for a box which she placed on the bed. Next she kicked a couple of empty boxes out of the way. When had she become the sort of person who kicked stuff out of her way? She strode to the chest of drawers and carried across some more clothing. Underwear, this time. Did she even mind me being here while she did this? What the hell was going on?

"I helped you get your stuff here," I said. "How are you going to move everything on your own?"

Because I'd be damned if I'd help her do it. No way could I lift boxes and furniture for her when my chest felt like it was about to cave in, my heart breaking.

"I'll manage," she said.

"Why? Why?" Tearing my hair out now. I pulled myself together. If she was going to 'manage', then so was I.

I gritted my teeth. "Where are you gonna go, Scarlett?"

She didn't look up. "I'll stay at Lily and Nick's while they're in Hawaii. I've still got a key, and Lily won't mind."

"And after they come back?"

"I've got ten days to find somewhere. That's heaps of time."

"You've got it all worked out."

"Actually I don't, Joel. The only part I've worked out is the first step."

She stopped, wiped a tear from her cheek. My heart stopped. I didn't want to see her in pain but if she was crying, that had to be a good sign, right?

Rimmed with red, her eyes had lost their sparkle. I remembered it so well, the way her face would light up with her eyes gleaming. For me. Her shoulders sagged, her clothes hanging off her as if she'd lost weight overnight. She didn't want this anymore than I did. She couldn't.

I held her gaze. "You don't have to do this. You can stay here."

Silence. It gave me time. Silence meant I had a chance.

"We've set up your studio," I said. "You still need somewhere to work, peace and quiet so you can concentrate, room to spread yourself out. It's a wonderful space, and you can't run a business without it."

She twisted her mouth. "The studio…"

A weak spot. My heart rate rose. Maybe we could keep this one connection. It'd be a start. We could begin all over again, a fresh start, maybe that would do the trick.

"I'm not using it," I said. "So there's no problem."

She pressed some clothes down into a box. "It won't last."

"How can you say that?"

"Well, what happens when you get another girlfriend? You won't want me hanging around outside, coming in to make coffee, looking out of the studio window while you're on the patio."

I spread my arms. "Who said anything about another girlfriend?"

"It'll happen. It's only a matter of time."

How could the overwhelming desire I'd felt for this woman have turned to such despair? How had we come to this?

I stepped closer, joining her on the other side of the bed. I'd been waiting for the right moment but there wasn't one. There was only now.

I held her gaze. "I love you."

"It's too late for that." Her voice cracked.

"It's never too late."

Tears filling her eyes, she turned away.

I reached for her hand, felt the warmth of her fingers in mine. "Maybe you care for me too."

"It's not enough."

She turned to glare at me, her eyes still filled with tears. And with fire. I let go of her hand, took a step back, wondered what the hell to do next.

Pulling her shoulders back, she looked around, then reached for the lid of the box. "There's no need for you to hang around. You must have things to do."

"Nothing nearly as important as talking to you."

"You're a busy guy, Joel, a workaholic. You've probably got thousands of things to do."

"Only a resignation letter to write."

Her mouth fell open. "So soon?"

"I couldn't give a shit about the job now, Scarlett. The only thing I care about is you, and you're leaving."

Her lower lip trembled but she straightened, holding her head high, then got back to the task at hand.

"I love you, Scarlett."

She wouldn't even look at me, probably didn't even believe me. Why would she when I'd waited till a moment of desperation to come out with it?

"I thought this was the best weekend of my life," I said. "It's turned into the worst. I've got all this time on my hands all of a sudden and I don't know what the fuck to do with it. I don't want anything else. I only want you."

She stared. Probably didn't appreciate the swearing, and I probably didn't care. She gave a curt shake of the head, one small movement that said so much and cut me to pieces.

I turned and left. Didn't come out with the old line about how if she left there was no coming back. That was way too banal. And also not true.

Because I'd take her back in a flash.

CHAPTER SIXTEEN

Scarlett

I lugged my suitcase up the front path of Lily's place, the house that had been mine once too. I needed a home, somewhere I fit and felt comfortable, somewhere to hide.

Nick's car sat in the driveway, which meant they must've taken a cab to the airport. It was probably cheaper than paying for ten days' parking, not that money was an issue for Nick, but Lily would always take the sensible option.

I put down the case, stabbed my key into the front door lock, and turned it, then heard shuffling noises from inside. My heart sank.

"Someone's here." Thomas's high-pitched voice sailed through the air.

I pressed my eyes shut. Too late to turn back. I hadn't wanted to intrude on them, hadn't wanted any of this to turn out this way.

Nudging the door open, I stayed behind the threshold. "Hello."

Nick yanked the door open, his mouth falling open as he put down the suitcase in his hand. "Scarlett?"

Another suitcase sat by the wall behind him. The place was overloaded with them.

I nodded. "Yep."

"We were just…"

"I'm sorry, Nick. I must've got the times wrong. I thought you guys had gone already."

"Not quite. Like I said, we were…"

Lily came up behind him, pulled his arm back to peer across, then got a better look at me and frowned. "Scarlett, what's…?" Glancing down at my suitcase, her face fell. "That's… Oh… Come on in, honey."

She pushed past Nick and wrapped her arms around me. I hugged her right back, held her close, then dredged up a smile as I broke the embrace.

"I was just apologizing to Nick," I said.

She shook her head. "You don't need to be sorry for anything."

"I was going to call you, honestly, as soon as I could. I was hoping I could stay here for a few days while you're away."

"Of course you can."

Nick nodded in agreement, probably too scared to speak, and I couldn't blame him. Not too frightened to reach for my suitcase and lift it to the rear of the hallway, though.

"Joel and I have broken up," I added.

Lily went in for another hug, marginally quicker this time.

"It's okay, really." I held her at arms' length. "I'll be fine, especially now I have somewhere to stay."

Lily pressed a hand to her temple. "Do you need to talk? We can take a later flight? We'll work something out."

"No, no." I ached to pour my heart out to Lily, the one person who'd understand, but waved it off. "Don't be silly. I can call you later."

Thomas's voice rang through the air. "Mommy, I found my car. It was right where you said." He came hurtling down the hall, a toy clutched in one hand, his Spiderman backpack over his shoulders. "Look, it's Auntie Scarlett. Are you visiting? Or are you going to be living with us again? Yay!"

"Hey." I crouched down to his level. "You need to give me a hug and then you need to make sure you're ready. You're going on a plane, remember?"

He nodded. "To Hawaii. And there's gonna be a water slide and volcanoes and all kinds of stuff."

"That's right." I gave him a hug, then stood to face the newlyweds. Guilt rocked through me at getting between them like this. "You look like you were on your way out. I can give you a ride if you like. It's no trouble."

"Thanks but we've already ordered a cab," Nick said. "And you look like you need to rest."

I stood tall, holding Nick's gaze. "I hope this won't change your opinion of Joel. He's an amazing bass player and he's committed to the band. He's perfect for you, no doubt about it. Anything that's happened between me and him is irrelevant."

All of which was true. He was committed. To The Merchants. A pang shot through my heart.

Nick held a hand out. "No problem. Don't worry, Scarlett. He's only just been accepted into the band. We're not gonna dump him."

"You guys go off and have a fabulous time." I hoped

the brightness in my voice didn't sound too forced.

Nick took Thomas's hand, picking up the suitcase with his other. "There's the cab. Good luck, Scarlett. You're welcome to stay here as long as you need. Or the apartment, if you prefer. Keys are in the fruit bowl." Then to Lily. "We'll meet you out there."

"Have a great time, guys," I yelled as they left.

Lily opened her mouth to speak but I couldn't bear the sympathy, couldn't stand being such a hindrance.

I got in quickly. "I don't want to ruin your honeymoon, Lily. You should go."

She tilted her head, thought about it. I knew exactly what would convince her.

"Look," I said. "I've been through worse. If I could get over Ronan screwing around on me, I can get over anything. I'll be fine."

It took all my strength to tell that lie. Ronan's unfaithfulness had nearly killed me, sucked the life right out of me, made me question my very worth. That part was true. There was a difference though, a big one. As long as it had taken to get over Ronan's betrayal, somehow I'd known deep down that he wasn't the guy for me and life would go on.

Lily was about to go in for another hug, when I pointed out onto the street. "You can't leave them waiting."

"Okay, honey." She picked up her suitcase, smaller than the one Nick had carried. "Take care of yourself."

A quick kiss on the cheek and she was off. I closed the door behind her because the longer I spent looking at them, the more energy this took, something I was running out of.

I wandered into the living room on shaking legs, relieved for the chance to sit down. I'd loaded up my car with boxes before leaving Joel's. They'd have to wait until I had my head together. And I'd have to go back for the next carload as soon as I'd brought those into the house.

My skin prickled as if there was something strange about the place, some sort of unusual presence, which was weird because I'd come here for the familiarity and comfort.

Then it hit me. I had it the wrong way round. The anticipation I felt was down to an absence of something, the complete lack of noise, the scarcity of people in the house.

When I'd lived here with Lily, Thomas was usually running around or playing quietly on his own but there'd always been some sort of background noise.

Instead, only silence. A resounding reminder that it was over.

CHAPTER SEVENTEEN

Joel

I stared at the wall in the band room at The Swamp, the wall that'd been black not so long ago. No windows in here so I'd set up a couple of spotlights to provide the light I needed to work on the mural, a ladder to one side, paints and a pallet laid out on a table. I'd spent a week on this, and it was coming along.

The life I'd always dreamed of. Supposedly.

I'd given my notice at work effective immediately, knowing George would be ready to step in. My boss had whooped when I'd told him, then proceeded to tell me he couldn't have been more thrilled, or more jealous. A guitar player himself, he knew exactly where I was coming from.

Meanwhile George hadn't been able to stop grinning because he'd been dying to run the design team for years. Other reactions in the studio varied from shock and surprise to polite congratulations.

Which just went to show that 'work' would always go on. Men often acted as if their jobs were life and death, but they weren't.

People mattered. Families counted. And relationships.

I was never going to lie on my deathbed wishing I'd spent more time at work and I was sure as shit never going to regret joining The Merchants.

But Scarlett… That particular regret would live on.

Painting had been my dream too. I loved to paint, something I'd never had enough time for. Now I had complete artistic freedom to let it rip on this huge fucker of a wall in a place that was better than an art gallery because it'd be filled with 'my people', band people, those who appreciated rock music in all its wonderful forms.

And when I wasn't here, I was rehearsing with The Merchants, a couple of hours at a time whenever the guys called me.

Yep, too good to be true. If not for the constant tugging in my gut.

A knock at the door behind me, I turned, my heart melting at the sight of her, my mouth suddenly dry. She closed the door, staying back as if waiting for permission.

"Hi." The best I could come up with.

Scarlett's lips curved to a wan smile as she ambled closer, not too fast, still tentative. A red dress hugged her curves, the skirt floating loose around her legs as she walked, each step bringing her closer. How could one person look so wonderful and terrible at the same time?

The red dress. A flash of inspiration. Scarlett, a color and a person all at once. I'd always thought her a beacon and now I knew exactly how to add the finishing touches to the mural.

Hope rippled through me. Sometimes that was all you needed, just a glimmer.

"Wow." Standing beside me, her eyes widened as she took in the mural. "That's amazing."

"Thanks."

"I've seen the painting you did at The Silver Swallow but this is so much bigger in every way. It's so cool." She pointed. "Look, up there you've got Nick and the guys taking center stage." In a small voice, she added, "But not you?"

"Not yet." I knew exactly where I was going to add myself to the mural and it wouldn't be what she was thinking at all. "I wanted to capture the Frankston music scene, people who've played here, and also the vibe of the place. Because The Swamp and the music that comes out of this town has a style of its own. An indie feel. Something unique. And I wanted the mural to embrace that, to show the character of what's gone on, and also to be a part of it."

"You've captured that, and more. I love the play of light and shade, the way the blacks, whites, and grays work together, and then you've thrown in just a touch of silver metallic. This is truly mind-blowing." She pointed to the blank space I'd been leaving for last. "What's going there?"

"Perhaps a splash of color." More likely a torrent, tidal wave, a tsunami, something to knock her over. Still, no way could she guess.

She raised her eyebrows. "And how are you finishing the edges?"

The mural sat in the middle of the wall because I had a very particular vision and didn't want to dilute my ideas by spreading the painting across the entire width of the wall. So, for the time being, the edges were ragged. It finished where it finished.

I said, "I'm thinking of bronze paint with shading to make it look like a chunky burnished frame."

"That'd really finish it off. Joel, I can't believe you've done all this in only a week. It's huge."

I couldn't believe it either, except I knew exactly what had gone into it. Forget about blood, sweat, and tears. I'd poured my gut into this mural, my heart too, though there was one small piece I was waiting to use.

"I didn't know you'd be coming in or I might have dressed for the occasion." I smiled, looking down at my paint splattered jeans and T-shirt.

"You don't need to worry about that. You look just fine."

Great, I looked 'fine' while she was a complete bombshell in that red dress. She'd barely looked at me. It was probably easier for her to stare at the mural and keep the conversation neutral.

I didn't want to be neutral. I wanted to be her everything.

She cleared her throat. "I came in to meet with Austin."

Of course. She hadn't dropped by to see me at all. My heart fell a little further.

"He stopped by earlier," I said. "Didn't mention anything about you coming in."

"He, uh, said you were kind of preoccupied."

"That's probably an understatement. When I get into the zone, I don't notice much else around me."

Which suited me because if my mind was free, it wandered only in one direction. To thoughts of Scarlett. And that had been killing me. Painting was my therapy, a self-protection mechanism, and pretty much all I had.

Scarlett had a life too, a new business she was starting.

I turned to her. "Hang on, if you've been meeting

Austin, does that mean…?"

"Yep, he's asked me to come on board and help out with the interior. So I've been ordering the light fixtures and loose furniture, all the items he's not so familiar with. And the banquettes, of course. I've been dealing with the carpenter for the framework and the upholsterer for the soft furnishings, pulling the different trades together. I'll be coming into the bar weekly from now on, to meet with the builders and make sure everything is on track."

Meanwhile I'd be done here soon. Like Scarlett and I were done. Except we weren't.

"I'm glad it's worked out for you," I said.

"The council approvals came through so now it's full steam ahead while Nick's away."

"I heard."

"So, yes, I'm keeping busy."

Like me. Only I didn't know if she was doing it for the same reasons.

"You haven't been working from your new studio though at my place, have you?" I asked.

Lips thin, she shook her head.

I cleared my throat. "So you've been working from home?"

"From Nick and Lily's place, yes. I took my files and samples and the other things I needed from the studio when you weren't there."

I'd noticed. Gritting my teeth, I nodded for her to continue.

"I'll come back another time for the furniture. Nick and Lily will back in a couple of days. I-I've found a small apartment."

My gut clenched. "Is that what you want?"

"Well, I don't want to impose on Nick and Lily anymore." She stepped away, pretended to look at the mural some more. "You've sure been busy. This is a big project."

"I've taken ownership of it," I said. "I wouldn't want to let Nick down. Or myself. I'm willing to put in the hard work when it matters."

I avoided the C word—commitment—but surely she could hear it in my voice. Yet in her eyes, the only thing I saw was reluctance.

She bit her lip, took a step back. "I'll leave you to it."

My heart ached as she walked to the door because she did it with such apparent ease, while I was yearning for any small sign she might come back.

"You don't have to, you know," I called out.

She stopped by the door. "Don't have to what?"

"You don't have to leave."

Her lower lip trembled, I hoped with hesitation. Instead she pushed the door open and walked away.

But I'd seen the glimmer I was looking for. Scarlett, my muse. I'd painted on and off for a long time but I'd never had a muse before. Had never known it could work this way.

I sat down with pencil and sketchpad to get my vision down on paper first. Then I'd mark the outline out in chalk on the black wall, as I'd done with the other images when composing the mural.

Scarlett, the red dress. A splash of color. I had my inspiration.

*   *   *

Another knock at the door. Tara called out, asking if she could enter.

"Come in." I stayed slumped in a chair, staring at the mural.

I'd gotten to know the bar manager even better over the last week. I might've been consumed by my painting, but she'd made a point of popping in regularly.

"It's after closing," she said.

"I know."

"You look like you're ready for bed." She glanced down at me, then across at the wall. If she'd noticed anything, she wasn't giving it away. "I thought you were working on the mural."

"I am. I'm thinking."

"About what?"

I turned to her. "It's all a part of the creative process. You mull things over, let the ideas fly around in your head, and sometimes the ideas feel like they've come out of nowhere, but they haven't. They pop into your head because they're at the back of your mind somewhere and you've been pondering. Nothing comes from nothing."

Tara placed a hand on her hips, tilted her head. "Looks like you've already been pretty creative if you ask me."

Okay, she'd noticed.

Silence, then, "Have you bought a ring?"

I jerked upright. Shit, I'd been so busy, so preoccupied, so focused on this one thing. What had I been thinking?

She must've seen the look on my face because she added, "Honey, you gotta buy a ring."

No, in fact, I didn't. Still, she was on the right track. I knew just the thing. Grandma's ruby ring from India, sitting untouched in the carved wooden box Gramps had given me. Mom had given me the ring years ago, along with some other jewelry, and Alex had received his share too. I remember his fiancée hadn't been interested in any of that old stuff.

But I knew exactly who would covet a ring like that. I hoped.

CHAPTER EIGHTEEN

Scarlett

I stared at the doors leading to the band room, a red ribbon with an enormous bow looped through the entry pulls. Joel wasn't playing tricks on me, I could tell that much, but the bow said one thing and the lack of people around us said another.

"You said this was a grand opening?"

Joel nodded.

I raised my eyebrows. "Of the band room?"

"Yep."

"So where is everyone? It's not like a surprise party when I pull open the door and everyone will jump up from behind the tables and yell out 'surprise'. Is it?"

"Nothing like that. Everyone who matters is painted on the wall. You'll see."

He handed me the scissors. I took them, my hand trembling, anxiety rippling through me at fear of the unknown, which was silly. I'd already seen the nearly completed artwork. It was the middle of the day, nothing to be afraid of. What could possibly go wrong?

I snipped through the ribbon, watching it fall to the

floor as Joel pulled the door open for me. I hated leaving mess on the floor, but stopped myself from picking it up. I'd learned at least this much from my time with Joel.

His hand on the small of my back, he ushered me into the darkened room, then strode ahead to switch on the spotlights he used for painting.

The mural looked more finished than before. He'd added further silver metallic highlights that shimmered over the blacks, whites, and grays of the artwork. And he'd completed the bronze frame. For some reason, he'd placed a ladder covered with a sheet in front of part of the mural.

"And champagne?" I pointed to a bottle in an ice bucket.

Champagne at two o'clock in the afternoon? What the hell was going on?

He pulled me closer. "There's something I'd like you to see."

I stood in front of the mural while he slid the ladder to one side, revealing the full size and scope of the mural. And something else.

My heart stopped, my hand flying to my mouth.

It was me. My red dress jumped out at me, the only color painted on the wall. With Joel in front of me. Joel on one knee, a small box in his hand, a ring box.

"Is that?" I gasped. "I-I…"

My knees felt suddenly weak, my head swaying. I knew what that meant, yet couldn't take it in. Couldn't comprehend. This was Joel, but the Joel I knew would never do something like this.

He pulled a chair closer. "You need to sit down."

A hand on my chest, I dropped down.

I needed to sit. I needed air. I needed a lot of things.

Crouching down in front of me, he took my hand into his and held my gaze. "I've changed, Scarlett. My life has changed since I met you. I've thought about this a lot. It's all I've thought about since you left. I want you back. I want to be with you tomorrow and the day after that and the year after that, the decade after that. Forever. Always. For keeps. Commitment."

"Joel, I-I…"

I can't speak. I don't know what to say. I'm too frightened to believe.

I looked down at our intertwined hands. "This is so quick."

"Three weeks, three months, three years. Doesn't matter how much time has passed. I know what I'm feeling on the inside is real and that it'll last."

He reached into his back pocket for a bundle of tissue paper that he held in his hands and slowly unwrapped it. A ring. My pulse skyrocketed, my heart thundering in my chest. Did I dare? Could I?

Sliding onto one knee, he took my hand back into his, holding the ring out to me.

"I love you, Scarlett. Will you marry me?"

I opened my mouth but nothing came out. Meanwhile every nerve ending in my body was on edge, my hands trembling, my heart ready to explode.

He held my hand tenderly. "I want to spend the rest of my life with you. Tell me you feel the same. Will you be my wife?"

"Yes," I whispered the word, realized I'd finally said it, then sucked some air into my lungs and yelled, "Yes!"

Joel slid the ring onto my finger, an antique ruby ring, so elegant and refined. My heart was still stammering in my chest as he pressed a gentle kiss to my lips.

"Yes," I said again.

He wrapped his arms around me, pulled me close. "Good, because there's no changing your mind."

Tears slid down my face. Where had they come from? I'd never been so happy to be crying my heart out.

I'd never been so happy. Ever.

CHAPTER NINETEEN

Joel

I knocked on the door of Scarlett's studio and let myself in. She looked up from her desk and smiled that beautiful smile I got to see about a hundred times a day. And it was staying that way.

"Ooh, coffee, how did you guess?"

I pressed a kiss to her cheek as I put the mug down. "I know when a woman's in need."

She smirked. "How gallant."

"Yep, your knight in shining armor." I perched against her desk. "Just because I play in one of the biggest rock bands in the country doesn't mean I can't stretch to making the occasional coffee."

"Or cleaning the bathrooms."

"I already did that." I folded my arms. "Trust you to bring me down to earth. I'm serious, though. I never want you to think I'm more important than you because I play in a band. Your work is every bit as important as mine."

She glanced across at her laptop. "I can't believe how busy it's become all of a sudden. I didn't even have to go looking for work. The jobs have come pouring in."

"I guess it was meant to be."

Her old boss, Margaret, had given Scarlett all her back pay plus a bonus to make up for what had happened too. Just as well.

She sipped her coffee, stretching out her fingers as she put the mug down. "I still love the ring. In case you were wondering."

"You don't have to love it. Like I said before, we could buy you a new one."

"No way."

How amazing that my grandmother had purchased such a beautiful ring and passed it on. The ruby in an antique setting was perfect for Scarlett in every way and suited her perfectly. I was glad she liked it. Beyond glad, actually.

"I thought you were working on that new song," she said.

"I am. I thought I'd take a break."

Maybe I'd used up all my inspiration on the mural and had to recharge my creative batteries. It was easier to spend my time learning the bass lines of The Merchants' songs. And practicing. You didn't get anywhere if you didn't practice.

We'd had a couple of rehearsals and had a bunch more lined up. I still couldn't believe I was in The Merchants of Menace. And in a couple of months we'd be playing The Falls Festival. Not playing. Headlining. I'd played at The Falls before, and there was a big difference.

"I thought you'd be working," Scarlett said.

"Hey, are you trying to get rid of me?"

"Never."

She stood and gave me a peck on the cheek, then

stared through the window at the yard. Despite the fact everything dried up in summer, it didn't look too bad. Maybe I was biased but, to me, the whole world looked fantastic.

"You sure you don't mind going to my parents' place for dinner again?" I asked.

"Are you kidding? I love curry and your mom's a fantastic cook. What's not to like?"

I pulled her closer. "My mom absolutely adores you. It means a lot to me."

"The most important thing is 'us'." Scarlett pressed a quick kiss to my lips. "Because I love you."

"Love you too."

I never knew it could be this way.

Keep reading for a sneak preview of Book 5…

ACKNOWLEDGMENTS

First of all, a big thanks to my very own rock star and in-house consultant, James.

Thanks very much to the people I interviewed, all experts in your particular fields and very patient with my dumb questions—Jenny Kim, Brooke Lundy, Scott Wilson, Brendan Murphy and Jo Taylor. Thanks heaps, guys!

And of course thanks to my fabulous critique partners, Claire, Lorraine, Juanita, Teena and Anna.

ABOUT THE AUTHOR

Susanna Rogers is the author of rock star romances for adults and kick butt books for young adults. Inspired by her very own in-house rock star and years of going to gigs, she penned the Mosh Series after writing and releasing several young adult novels. She's also a kickboxer and dreams of empowering girls and guys around the globe to believe in themselves, to take care and follow their own dreams. She has a soft spot for romantic suspense, also with kick butt heroines, so you never know what might be coming up next.

She would love to hear from you—susannarogers.com.

If you like her books, please post a review on Amazon or Goodreads. She'd like that a lot.

LIGHT & SHADE
MOSH BOOK 5

CHAPTER ONE

Cooper

Guys weren't supposed to get emotional at weddings, everyone knew that. So why the tightness in my throat, the weakness in my legs even though I was sitting down?

I knew the reason. Didn't mean the rest of the world needed to know too.

Jess leaned closer. "Nick looks so nervous."

Shifting from foot to foot, he stood down the front, facing the white chairs that'd been laid out for the guests in his parents' enormous garden, with best man Lachie at his side.

"Don't you think, Cooper?" Jess asked more loudly.

"Yeah, sure does."

I sucked in a long, slow breath. Hell, all I had to do was make it through the ceremony and I'd be fine. It wasn't as if I was the one getting married. Besides, I'd known Nick and Lily since high school, and they had a kid together. The only surprise was that Nick had finally come to his senses and seen what had been in front of his eyes the whole time.

Meanwhile I was having a small problem with my own eyes. Couldn't get them off the photographer. Where on earth had Nick found her? Or maybe she was a friend of Lily's. And why hadn't I already met her or at the very least seen her around?

I struggled to get a good view as the young woman crouched down near the front, camera raised, a few strands of dark hair escaping from her hair-do, the smooth skin of her neck exposed, her black dress cupping her butt. Black. For a wedding. How perfect. Black had never looked so bright or beautiful.

She straightened, tugged the skirt down with one hand, the dress clinging in all the right places. There were no wrong places.

My pulse rising, I wiped the perspiration from my brow. Nothing to do with her. I blamed the Nevada heat.

Coming to my senses, I saw Joel heading down the aisle. Our new bass player. On his own. We couldn't have that. He'd been talking to Nick and Lachie down the front and I'd barely even noticed.

I stepped into the aisle. "Hey, why don't you join us?"

Joel stopped. "Sure."

He asked Jess if she'd prefer the aisle seat for a better view, such a gentleman. I needed to get my shit together. At the very least, I should introduce them.

"This is Jess." I laughed. "We're the leftovers."

Joel hadn't been in the band long enough to meet Jess, Lachie's partner, so I explained who she was. And said I was simply left over.

She gave me a quick whack. I rubbed my shoulder. Honestly, that girl didn't know her own strength.

"No, you're not," she said. "All it means is you haven't found the right girl yet, Cooper."

Maybe she was wrong about that. I swallowed. Didn't

dare turn around to look for the photographer or I'd give away too much.

Polite chat, I could do polite chat. Besides, talking about Jess and explaining how she was a bodyguard was much safer than any discussion about me. I had too much going on at the moment and wasn't ready to go there. I'd only be able to hide it for so long, though.

Glancing toward the aisle, I saw the gorgeous photographer pointing her camera in our direction.

I thrust my hand out. "No, no thanks."

Not now. I hoped that didn't sound like panic in my voice. The band might be called The Merchants but I was absolutely not a panic merchant. I just didn't like having my photo taken so much lately.

Jess called out, and as she motioned for the young woman to join us, my heart rate rose again. And we hadn't even spoken yet. What the hell was going on with me?

"Love the dress," Jess said to her. "You look like a Korean Audrey Hepburn."

Korean, that explained the exotic looks, but what could explain that incredible combination of bombshell and demure? The breath left my body.

She left us, heading down the front, probably preparing to take photos of the bride as she walked down the aisle.

Joel turned to Jess. "So, you know Ginger?"

"Yeah," she said. "She's a friend of my housemate's."

"And she's the official photographer?"

"Yep."

Ginger. I had a name now. And by the end of the night I hoped to have a lot more than that.

I leaned closer to Jess. "Has she always lived here?"

"Yep." She screwed up her nose. "You've been away too long."

But I was back. With a vengeance. Twenty-five years old and I'd come home to stay.

Familiar notes rang out from the piano. I knew the song. We all did. I'd wondered about the baby grand over to the side. Now I had my answer.

The chords tugged at my heart, my response immediate and undeniable. It was what music did, the reason I played in a band, even if a lot of people thought drummers weren't true musicians.

Nick, the world's biggest Paul McCartney fan, started singing *Maybe I'm Amazed*. Our singer could belt out the biggest rock songs, could do a devil's scream to rival the best, and he could melt hearts of solid metal when he sang a beautiful melody. Like now. It was enough to make a grown man cry.

We all stood as young Thomas the ring bearer and Lily's sister came down the aisle, followed by the bride herself. If only Nick would stop singing that song, if only the words weren't so damn meaningful, if only the melody wasn't so gut wrenching. If only...

Don't think about it, Cooper. Don't think about anything.

So I got into the zone, the strange place I took myself when things got too much for me, because there was only so much one person could cope with and I had a hell of a lot on my plate at the moment. *At the moment*. Who was I kidding? As if things were going to get better.

But I couldn't let myself mope. Refused to sulk. Hell, I'd already done enough brooding to last a lifetime.

The rest of the ceremony followed the usual plan, the exchange of vows, the first kiss as husband and wife, then walking down the aisle together with their son, Thomas. Somehow Ginger made time between taking photos to say something to make the kid laugh and give him a fist bump.

I didn't have to wait long to congratulate the bride and groom. Nick saw me and opened his arms for a bear hug. We'd been through a lot together—as a band, as friends, and as two young guys who were constantly fucking up.

And now he was on to the next stage of his life. I held him at arms' length, my heart swelling for all the right reasons because I couldn't have been happier for him.

His lower lip trembled as he looked at me. I didn't want anything resembling pity and, besides, this was his big day. I turned to Lily instead, kissed her on both cheeks.

"I wish you every happiness," I said to her, before turning to Nick. "And you, Nick, are one lucky bastard!"

The two of them laughed.

I mingled and mixed, acting like the perfect guest. I kept an eye out for Ginger who seemed to be acting like the perfect photographer, taking plenty of photos, making Thomas giggle, giving people space when they needed it. Keeping her distance from me, it seemed too. Or maybe I was reading too much into it.

I'd give it time. Not too much, but I didn't want to annoy her when she was in full swing with the photography. Timing was everything.

Bridesmaid Scarlett came up and kissed Joel on the lips, the two of them practically radiating joyfulness. Standing nearby, I was ready to join them when a passing waiter offered me a glass of champagne.

I shook my head. "Do you have any mineral water?"

"Certainly, sir."

He came back a minute later with a San Pellegrino. I

knocked back half the bottle. Must've been thirstier than I'd thought.

Yep, I told myself it was refreshing, thirst quenching, everything I could've wanted. Usually I didn't miss alcohol. This was different though, a celebration, one of those times when mineral water didn't cut it.

Joel was keen to chat since we were now in a band together, and I wanted to get to know him better too. Other people mingled while the bridal party wandered off to another part of the garden for photographs.

"This place is really something." Joel looked around.

"Yeah, isn't it?"

Nick's parents' house was a mansion, bigger than anything else I'd seen when I was growing up, the garden so large it was separated into different immaculately landscaped sections.

"I know what you mean," I said. "They've got a tennis court in their back yard. When I was a kid that used to amaze me. Still does."

"Came in handy, though."

"Sure did." They'd set the wedding marquee up on it.

Scarlett came back later, bringing Austin with her. So strange seeing the two guys together, our old bass player with the new one. Austin was happy with his decision to leave the band, with the new life he was building for himself, and especially with his new woman.

Happiness. You couldn't argue with that. What else mattered in the end?

Scarlett turned to me. "I'm on a mission. I need you to come over with us and have your photo taken. Nick wants a picture with all the guys from the band."

"Sure." I figured there'd be safety in numbers.

So we made our way to a secluded garden with a rockery and waterfall for the photographs.

Ginger was concentrating on the camera on its tripod, nodding and frowning at the same time, probably thinking of her next shot. Such a pretty frown. Man, I hadn't even known a frown could look so cute.

Lily waved and Nick called out, "Over here."

I joined them. We had a photo to take, and with Lachie and Austin in place next to them, I didn't want to be the one holding everybody up.

If I wasn't mistaken, Ginger was checking me out, watching me, perhaps because I'd turned down a photo before. But this was different, a group shot for old times sake. And for Lily.

We got in place for a formal photograph with the bride in the middle and two of us guys on either side.

Ginger took a couple of shots, then sized us up, a sneaky expression on her face. "Great, but can we get something that's a bit more rock 'n' roll."

I looked at Nick, then the others, saw the glint in their eyes and worked out exactly what they were thinking. I nodded, gave the signal, and Nick swept Lily up in his arms. She shrieked, then giggled as the four of us held her across us horizontally like something out of a teen movie. Laughing, natural, mucking around, this was 'us'.

We weren't done yet, though, Afterwards, I got down on one knee, resting my arm on my leg and putting on a fake suave expression, with Lachie and Austin following suit. We'd spent enough time fooling around together to know how to ham it up.

Ginger clicked away with the camera. "Lachie, can you come forward a bit."

Someone handed me a rose from the garden. I put it between my teeth like a Spanish conquistador. If Ginger wanted a good pose, I'd give her one. Right now, I'd give her pretty much anything she wanted.

She gave us the thumbs up when she was done, then the three of us slowly got to our feet. I kept my distance while Ginger took more photos of the bride and groom. Lachie was talking to Joel who looked ready to explode with happiness, making me wonder what was going on.

Lachie left him and Scarlett in a rapturous hug, came over to me, and explained that Nick hadn't gotten around to telling Joel, our new bass player, he was in the band. That was one hell of an oversight. Shit, if I'd known, I'd have told him myself.

I ambled across to Joel, whacked him on the shoulder, and told him pretty much that. Scarlett had already wandered off, probably for official bridesmaid's duties, so it was just the two of us.

"There are a few other things we need to fill you in on too." I swallowed the lump in my throat. There were some things it was better not to think about. Plenty of things. I added. "Maybe another day. Now we've got to celebrate."

So we had a celebratory drink while I talked and Joel seemed to be off the planet with elation.

After a while, I made my way toward Ginger, her hand still resting on the camera, her eyes on me as I came closer. Sultry, warm, brown eyes. Beautiful pale skin tones too. I tried to keep the hunger and the ache at bay. Hard to do when her beauty stole my breath.

"Hi Ginger." I stretched out my arm for a handshake, and cleared my throat because a trembling voice wouldn't make a good impression. "I'm Cooper McVeigh."

She squeezed my fingers, got up on tip toes and kissed my cheek. My lips touched her cheek too. I made sure they did.

Stepping back, she looked me up and down. "I know who you are. I've seen the band."

"I hope that means you like the music."

She gave a long slow nod. "A lot."

"That's good to hear."

"You know—" she paused, "—for someone who doesn't like having his photo taken, you did pretty well back there."

"I try. You caught me unawares earlier, that's all."

"I'm not like some paparazzi photographer following your every movement."

"No, I can't imagine you hiding in the bushes taking secret photos of me with a long lens while I'm taking a midnight skinny dip."

She gave me a sly smile. "I'd like to see that."

"You probably can if you Google it."

"Why would I Google when I've got the real thing in front of me?"

"Good point." I looked around. Nick and Lily were still here but most of the others had left, no doubt making their way to the reception.

Talk. I had to talk to her, keep the conversation going. "Do you do a lot of weddings?"

"A few. Mostly, I do commercial work."

"Such as?"

"Everything from advertising shots and wine bottles to headshots in boardrooms. The full range from photos of child care centers to aged care facilities. Pretty much anything anyone will pay me to photograph." She held my gaze and smiled. "I'm fussy like that."

Despite the smooth skin and serene expression, her smile appeared loaded. And maybe a little of what lay behind those curved lips was reserved for me.

"I've taken lots of photos of local bands too," she added.

"Not The Merchants, though?"

"It was a long time ago."

"What was? You've taken photos of us?"

Shock ripped through me. Surely I'd have remembered her, unless I'd had my head well and truly up my ass or if I'd been off my face. If it was long enough ago, either of those options was a distinct possibility.

"One of your early gigs," she said. "The shots were all taken from a distance from the side of the stage or shooting through the audience. I was trying to capture the feel from the crowd. I've still got the files if you're interested."

Right now I was interested in a lot of things. I had to know more. Had to see more.

I raised my eyebrows. "Maybe you could show me some time?"

"What? Like, come up and see my etchings? Isn't that an old line?"

"Nothing wrong with the old ways. I mean, you could email the images, but that wouldn't be quite so much fun."

"And you're all about enjoying yourself?"

"What's the point of living if you can't have a little fun from time to time?"

"True." She looked around. "But I'm working and need to move on to the reception."

"Sure."

Ginger slipped the lens cap onto the camera, crouching down while she placed it back in the camera bag and rearranged a couple of items. It gave me more of a chance to admire the curves of her hips and butt. Maybe a chance to catch my breath too.

She stood, folding the legs of the tripod and collapsing them together. Smooth, practiced movements. Long, lean legs. Toned arms and a beautiful curve to her neck. Hell, I could stand here all day.

I reached for the tripod, my hand brushing against hers. "Let me give you a hand with that."

"Ooh, I don't usually have a photographic assistant."

She handed it to me, then bent over and hoisted the camera bag over her shoulder, leaning to the other side so she didn't over balance.

"Let me take that instead," I said.

"But you're a guest."

"Come on, we'll swap." I held the tripod out to her. "I can handle it."

She bit her lip as if deliberating, then swung the camera bag in my direction. I lifted the strap over my shoulder, accidentally grunting as I did so. I didn't know how she managed with that thing. I guess that explained the muscles.

My hand on her lower back, I ushered her ahead of me. Such pretty shoulders exposed by the sleeveless dress, such a slender waist, such a gentle swing to her hips.

I'd wasted way too much time in my life doing dumb shit. Those days were over. I was turning over a new leaf, making the most of all the good things in my life, enjoying every moment.

And maybe one of those good things was right in front of me.